# SEALS

Tynan turned and could see the aircraft above them, a distant plane barely visible in the dark, a high-wing craft with four turbo props that looked like an American-made C-130 Hercules.

Apparently the Cubans had spotted it too. There was a quick burst from one of the anti-aircraft guns ... The plane kept coming, the roar of the engines louder.

Tynan aimed his weapon at the anti-aircraft gun. He hesitated, but the gun began to fire again, short explosions, aimed at the incoming plane. Tynan returned the fire, a quick burst and then a longer one. He burned through the magazine. The last three rounds streaked out. Tracers told him the magazine was coming up on empty...

# CRISIS!

# SEALS

### #13

## CRISIS!

## STEVE MACKENZIE

AVON BOOKS ◆ NEW YORK

SEALS #13: CRISIS! is an original publication of Avon Books. This work has never before appeared in book form. This work is a novel. Any similarity to actual persons or events is purely coincidental.

AVON BOOKS
A division of
The Hearst Corporation
105 Madison Avenue
New York, New York 10016

Copyright © 1989 by Kevin D. Randle
Published by arrangement with the author
Library of Congress Catalog Card Number: 88-91367
ISBN: 0-380-75771-0

First Avon Books Printing: May 1989

AVON TRADEMARK REG. U.S. PAT. OFF. AND IN OTHER COUNTRIES, MARCA REGISTRADA, HECHO EN U.S.A.

Printed in the U.S.A.

K-R   10   9   8   7   6   5   4   3   2   1

# 1

It was raining hard, coming down in grey-white sheets that hid the parking lot lights and the cars there. People were grouped around the windows, watching the rain hit the concrete and bounce eighteen inches high. The sidewalk was a river and the garden a lake. No one wanted to brave the storm. At least not until the rain had slackened and they could see their destinations, no more than thirty or forty feet away.

Navy Lieutenant Mark Tynan stood at the rear of the group, looking over the shoulders of those pressed against the window, their body heat steaming it and making it even harder to see out.

Tynan was a young man, nearing thirty, and stood just over six feet tall. He had brown hair and blue eyes that some claimed changed color with his moods. He was a wiry man, not burly, but strong and had been trained in various forms of unarmed combat, though he preferred to use a weapon, sometimes the silenced Browning M-35s the Seals normally carried or the M-16s that were being issued to everyone who'd carry it.

"Looks like it's going to wash away the base," said a voice.

Tynan turned and looked into the hard, steel blue eyes of a captain wearing his whites. There were five rows of ribbons above his pocket and not one of them a decoration for meritorious service.

"That and the whole town," agreed Tynan.

A car plunged out of the gloom, the headlights burning through grey of rain. It stopped, the black lettering on the door almost obscured by the rain.

"Looks like my ride," said Tynan.

"You sure, son? Could be for me."

Tynan grinned. "And now I'm detailed to run out there to find out."

"No. You just hang tight. The driver will come in to make an announcement if we're patient."

A moment later the driver dived through the door, dripping wet from the five yard sprint. Her dark brown hair, pinned up to keep it off her collar was soaked through. She was a Marine, in a green uniform tightly tailored to her trim body, the skirt ending above her knees. Two red stripes were sewn to the sleeves and she held a hand on her headgear as if a wind would snatch it from her, even inside the building.

"Lieutenant Tynan?"

The captain grinned and said, "Just my luck. I usually get old Chiefs who figure they know more than me and want to tell me all about it."

"Best of luck, Captain," said Tynan. He raised a hand. "I'm Tynan."

"This way sir."

"We in a big hurry, Corporal?"

She looked at Tynan and then back out the window where the rain still pelted down. A wind had picked up now and was driving it.

"No, sir. Not a big hurry."

"Then let's hang loose. Rain will slow up in a few minutes." He waited and then said, "The life of the average thunderstorm is about fifty minutes."

Another sailor laughed out loud. "I've seen them go all day long."

"Not the same storm," said Tynan. "A squall line can make it look as if a storm lasts for a couple of hours, but in truth it's one storm replacing another."

"So who the hell cares?" asked another of the men standing there.

Tynan turned his attention back to the corporal. "How'd you see to get here?"

"Wasn't so bad. I drove slow and watched the edge of the blacktop. It looked smoother than the rough sides."

"Christ!" yelled a voice. "If it doesn't stop soon, I'm building an ark."

The corporal looked at her watch. "Sir, we're going to be late if we don't hurry."

"Don't worry about it. It'll be my fault because I didn't want to get wet." Tynan smiled and then asked, "What's your name anyway?"

"Strong, sir. Deborah Strong."

"Well, Corporal Strong," said Tynan, "if you're game, I think we can make a run for it."

"Yes, sir."

They shouldered their way to the front door and looked out. The grey curtain had risen slightly and they could see out, into the parking lot, and even beyond, to where cars slipped by on the highway.

Tynan opened the door and felt warm, moist air on his face. He ducked his head and ran for the back door of the staff car, diving inside before he could get soaked. Strong used the passenger door and then scrambled across the front seat, shifting around so that she could sit behind the wheel. As she did, she tugged at the hem of her skirt, pulling it lower.

When she had the car running again, she turned and looked over the seat at Tynan in the back. "If you're ready sir."

"Go ahead."

They pulled away from the curb and Tynan glanced back, at the blaze of light on the front of the officer's club. Points of brightness, surrounded by a grey-white mist and circles of rainbow color. It faded away as the rain hammered at the car. Strong kept it moving slowly, watching for the signs and the cross streets.

As they moved across the base, Tynan could see little of it. There were hints of buildings seen through the sheets of rain. Lights in windows or on the fronts of the barracks. Open fields that were paved parking lots or parade grounds. And off to the left, the almost invisible lights of the airfield. Nothing was moving on it. At least not until the thunderstorm ended.

They worked their way deeper into the base and then stopped outside of a brick and concrete block structure surrounded by a chainlink fence twelve feet high that was topped with coils of barbed wire.

"You're supposed to go on in, sir," said Strong.

"What about you? Do you wait for me?"

"Yes sir. I was told to wait right here and take my orders from you."

Tynan slipped over to the door and grabbed the handle there. Before he opened it, he said, "I'll try not to be too long, but I really don't know what this is about."

"Don't worry, sir," she said. "I brought a book. A long one so I wouldn't be bored."

Tynan opened the door and jumped out into the rain. He ran for the gate, saw that it was closed and then noticed the

SEALS **5**

guard, wearing rain gear and carrying an M-16 standing near it.

As Tynan reached the gate, the guard said, "Name, sir?"

"Tynan, Mark. Lieutenant."

"Yes sir. You're on the list." He opened the gate and let Tynan enter. "You'll need to sign in when you get in."

"Thanks." Tynan now walked the rest of the way. He was drenched and there was no reason to run. He couldn't get any wetter.

There were double doors ahead of him with light bleeding through. Beyond them was a single man sitting at a table. He was in fatigues and wore a sidearm. Tynan opened the door, stepped into the coolness of an air conditioned room that seemed colder because he was rain wet.

"You have an ID card, sir?"

Tynan pulled out his wallet and flashed the green military ID. The sailor looked at the picture, up at Tynan and back at the picture. He grinned and said, "Not a real good likeness."

"Is yours?"

"No sir. I don't think my mother would recognize me in the picture." He twisted a clipboard around and said, "Sign in please."

Tynan did as instructed.

The sailor pointed down a darkened hallway. "Through the double doors and down the steps. Second door on the left. You won't be able to miss it because it's the only room being used at this time of night."

"Thanks." Tynan walked down the hallway, ignoring the pictures on the wall that showed the local chain of command in black and white. He opened the double doors, found a cement staircase and walked down, holding onto the grey, metal railing. He reached the bottom, turned and exited. There was light from only one room. He walked toward it, and stopped.

It was a large room with a conference table in the center of it. There were blue chairs surrounding it and there were people, men and women, sitting in some of them. The walls were painted a light green and there were maps hanging on one. Aerial photos, all in black and white and all blown up to huge sizes were displayed opposite the maps. A captain in blues stood at the head of the table. He was a short, stocky man with jet black hair, a permanent five o'clock shadow, and small eyes almost lost in his round face.

"Who're you?"

"Tynan, sir."

"Tynan? Ah yes. The SEAL."

Tynan nodded and said, "We try to keep that fact under wraps. It sounds melodramatic."

"Whatever. Have a seat. Coffee on the table over there, if you want any."

Tynan wasn't sure that he did, but he was cold. He moved, poured himself a cup and then sat down. He wanted to ask questions, but knew he'd get no answers until someone decided it was time to talk to him. The best move was to sit quietly and wait patiently.

A few minutes later, the captain who had been at the club walked in. Like Tynan, he was soaked. He saw Tynan, nodded and said, "If I had known you were coming here, we could have shared the ride."

"Yes sir."

The captain in blue took his seat then and said, "Now that we're all here, we can get started. Marcel, you want to close the door?"

When the door was closed, the captain looked around the room and said, "For those of you who don't know me,

I'm Captain Owens and I'll be ram-rodding this little operation. The information I'm about to give you is classified as secret. I'm trusting each of you to tell me if you have a current clearance and if not, to voluntarily leave the room." He scanned the faces one at a time and when no one moved, added, "Good. Let's get started. Commander Marcel, if you please."

Marcel moved toward the maps on the wall. He was a tall, thin man with salt and pepper hair. He wore a clean uniform with shoes that had been recently shined. It meant that he had either changed clothes after arriving, or had been in the building when the meeting was scheduled so that he didn't have to fight the rain.

Marcel looked at each of them and then turned to the map. "This doesn't show the island very well because it's such a small, insignificant place, but it does give you an indication of where it's located."

He pointed at the map, to a point southeast of Cuba and said, "These are the Lesser Antilles. A chain of islands that, when linked to the Greater Antilles almost link South America with Mexico. They define the Caribbean Sea and the Gulf of Mexico. They are made up of territories belonging to the United States, the United Kingdom and free nations. Most of them are small, poverty stricken and not worth the trouble it would take to overrun them in a military operation."

"Keep the opinions to yourself, Commander," advised the Captain.

"Yes sir." He pointed to a spot on the map that was barely visible and that looked more like a smudge than an island. "This, then, is Grande Terre de la Desirade."

"You have got to be shitting me," said the Captain who had been in the officer's club.

Marcel looked at the officer and grinned. "No sir. The Great Land of Desire."

The Captain laughed. "Jes-zus!"

Marcel picked up a hand drawn map and taped it over the real one. "The island is twelve miles long, four miles wide at the widest and looks like a fat peanut. The high point is four hundred and twelve feet above sea level, and there is a swamp or marsh near the center that is about ten feet below sea level. There is a single major city, San Antonio de la Desirade but called simply, San Antonio by everyone. About a hundred thousand people live there and there is a university situated on the outskirts."

"This is all quite fascinating," said the officer club Captain.

"Yes, sir," said Marcel ignoring the sarcasm. "And there is more. They have no military to speak of. The navy consists of five coastal patrol boats, a gift from our State Department. The army is also the police force. About five thousand men organized into an active police force of two thousand and three maneuver battalions of one thousand men each. They have no real heavy weapons with the exception of some old anti-tank guns and a battery of 105's. They are armed with Soviet made AK-47s, RPDs and RPGs."

Marcel moved away from the map, checked his notes and said, "Their air force is a single P-51 stripped of its guns and two C-47s, none of which seem to have gotten off the ground in the last three years."

He looked at the head of the table and said, "I can go into greater detail now, if you'd like."

"Thank you, no, Commander." Owens looked at the people assembled and said, "I think it gives us an idea about this place. A fourth rate little island empire with nothing of value on it except a bunch of poor people who think the United States and the rest of the world owes them something. Not worth a damn except for the port facilities."

"Then why is it suddenly so important that I have to leave my dinner, my wife and daughters and run through a thunderstorm to learn about it," asked the Captain.

"Because, we're going to invade it shortly," said Owens quietly.

# 2

The night was hot and muggy and with the electricity off
again, studying was impossible. First, it meant no air conditioning or fans and second it meant no lights. The lack of
lights could be fixed with the lanterns and flashlights that
everyone had, but the air conditioning couldn't be fixed. It
meant windows were open and the hot, sea air was blowing
in, filled with a smell of salt and fish, and coating everything with a fine, light mist that refused to dry.

It was hot and miserable, everyone agreed.

Ed Godwin gave it up just after nine o'clock. He
stripped his sweat soaked shirt and then his blue jeans,
replacing them with cut-offs. He grabbed a portable radio
and left the tiny room that held his cot, shelves made of
salvaged lumber and bricks, and a wardrobe jammed with
his clothes, and headed for the roof.

Up there he found most of the other students spread out.
A lantern was set up in the middle of the roof, looking like
a campfire on a beach. There were lawn chairs in a rough
circle, filled by boys and girls, one of them with a guitar.
They were singing quietly.

Across the roof, looking out over the ocean was another
group, standing and sitting and talking. Godwin walked

over to them, put a bare foot up on the three foot high wall and leaned an elbow on his knee.

"Think the power's gone for the rest of the night."

"Shit," said a voice. "I can't sleep in this heat. Can't study. Nothing to do."

A feminine voice said, "I bet we could think of something."

"Nope. Too hot. You get all sweaty and then your body slides around."

"I kind of like that."

"Well then maybe there is something to do."

Godwin shook his head. "That all you ever think about, McKinley?"

"Yes."

A shadow approached from the right. A small shadow with a distinctive hour glass shape. Godwin stared in the moonlight and starlight, could see the long, dark hair, the roundness of the face and the hips and knew it was Victoria Kehoe. Vicki, with an eye, said, "Hi," to everyone.

"Hi, Vicki."

"Hello. Give up the studying?"

"It was too hot and too cramped in the room."

She held out a can and said, "Want a beer?"

Godwin took it and drank, thinking that it was going to be some of the tepid local brew, but it was ice cold and tasted like the nectar of the gods. He held the can up and saw the Budweiser on the label.

"Where in the hell did you get this?"

"My brother worked on a fishing boat and he brought it to me. Figured a case or two would do me good."

"And how in the hell did he get it here? I would have thought his buddies would have drank it all before they swung this far south."

"He bought ten cases and only made it with two."

Godwin took another drink and felt better. He reached out and touched Kehoe on the shoulder. She turned and moved off, toward the other side of the building, staying away from the light of the lantern and the group of song-birds. She stopped at the edge and then sat on the wall.

Godwin followed her and put his foot up. Drinking the beer slowly, wanting to make it last, he scanned the horizon and the darkened city of San Antonio de la Desirade. Normally when the power failed, there were parts of the city still bathed in the yellow glow of artificial lights. The Presidential Palace, with its back-up generators, if nothing else, stood out like a beacon, but tonight even it was dark.

"I could really grow to hate it here," she said.

"What do you mean? This is a tropical paradise. People from Des Moines spend thousands of dollars just to visit places like this. They lay on the beach for legendary tans and dream about living out their lives here."

"Not here," she said. "Hawaii. The Virgin Islands. But not here."

"Not here," repeated Godwin.

"Look at you," she said. "Guarding that beer like it was something rare and precious."

"It is," said Godwin.

"No," snapped Kehoe. "It's a damned beer. Thousands of them are brewed everyday."

"What's your point?"

"I hate it here." She stopped talking for a moment and then said again, "I hate it. No electricity half the time. Lousy food. People who hate us." She pointed at the small radio that Godwin carried. "No rock and roll, just that reg-gae or steel drum shit they push because they invented it in Jamaica or whatever and now it's almost like a national treasure. One television station that mainly shows our leader telling us how great it is here or re-runs of *Dallas*."

Godwin nodded and finished his beer. "Maybe you should pack up and get out."

Kehoe shook her head. "I played too hard in college."

"Didn't we all," said Godwin. "If I had known that I'd end up in medical school here, I think I would have taken things just a little more serious. Now I'm stuck here for another couple of years."

"I'm stuck here too," she said.

Godwin drained the beer and crushed the can in his hand. He set it carefully on the wall. "If only we could tell all those screwing around in college now. Pay attention or you'll end up here."

"A little extra work," she said.

"Still, it could be worse. A couple of my friends screwed around and ended up in the Army. I, at least, managed to keep my student deferrment."

Kehoe laughed. "You've even less reason to be here than me. If I had a student deferrment and the possibility of the draft hanging over my head, I wouldn't be here. I'd be in the States, maybe not at Harvard or Johns Hopkins, but a better school than this one."

Now Godwin sat down on the wall, staring out into the night. Music from a radio drifted up to them, mixing with the singing coming from the group around the lantern. There was a quiet noise off to the right, south of the city that built slowly and became the screaming roar of jet engines.

Godwin glanced up and watched as the huge transport flew overhead. The navigation lights were blinking and it seemed that one door was open, red light bleeding out.

"What the hell?" he said.

Around him the music stopped and those near the lantern stood up, looking into the sky. Two more jets flew over them and turned to the west, away from the coast. As they crossed the city, nearing the airport no more than a mile from the campus, they slowed and the doors all popped open as paratroopers began tumbling into the night sky.

"What the hell?" said Godwin again.

In the rear of the lead aircraft Major Hector Salinas, stood off to one side and watched as his men, the first of his battalion, stood and hooked up to the static line for their jump. It was a ritual as old as the paratroops, with the men checking each other's equipment, making sure that each man had everything he was required to carry and that he had made the proper adjustments to the parachute that he wore. None of them had spare chutes because they were jumping too low. If the main didn't deploy, there would be no time for the reserve.

The roar of the engines cut back then, suddenly, and the light that had been burning red was suddenly green. Without an order, the first of the men hit the door and launched himself into space. The men moved forward rapidly, each following the other as they bailed out. Salinas was right behind them, stepping out into nothing but hot muggy air that was nearly impossible to breathe. The roar of the jets receded and below was the dark expanse of the airport with no lights glowing.

In only a few seconds Salinas was on the ground, his chute off and rolled into a ball at his feet. He pulled his weapon around and chambered a round. He dropped to one knee and waited as the other soldiers moved toward him, falling in line behind him.

Without a word, Salinas raised a hand and waved them forward. Two of them ran silently fifty yards and then slowed to a walk. The rest of the men got up, moving rapidly forward, toward the terminal building, hangars and control tower of the airfield. With the electricity out, all flights had been diverted to alternate airports on other islands. A four man team with bolt cutters, plastic explosives, and engineering degrees had infiltrated the powerplants forty minutes before the parachute drop to insure the power would be out all over the island.

Salinas and his soldiers hurried across the grass, through a row of tropical plants covered with bright flowers and huge, broadleaves. They fanned out and three men ran for the side door of the closest building. As they approached it, it opened and a single shape stepped out.

The men dived for the ground, freezing. Salinas slipped back, into the shadows, waiting for his men to take charge. One of them slipped to the right, hugging the shadows. As the man from the building moved to the rear, the soldier was up and moving. He hit the man from the rear, taking him down in textbook fashion. One arm around the throat, squeezing as he dragged the suspected enemy to the rear, onto the fulcrum of his knee to break the back. There was a muffled crack and the soldier rolled the body to the ground where it didn't move.

The soldiers moved forward then, running across the open ground. They reached the wall and used the shadows to conceal themselves. From somewhere came a burst of machine gunfire. A single ripping sound that shredded the night and then fell silent.

Salinas nodded and two men took the door, one of them opening it and the other diving through. For a second there was no sound and then a shout in Spanish. A gun fired and then another.

Salinas saw one man dive back out the door and the second staggered, took a round in the spine and hit the ground with a bounce. Fire erupted then. Muzzle flashes stabbed out, strobing like a camera with an automatic wind.

Salinas hesitated and then moved forward, his back against the rough stone of the wall. He nodded and one man ran forward, tossed in a grenade and then dived to the right. As the grenade exploded, another man dragged the wounded man out of the way.

Salinas dived through the open door, rolled and aimed his rifle, but didn't fire. One man inside, stood, weaving back and forth. He half-heartedly raised his weapon and Salinas fired. The man took the round in the chest and fell. He didn't move again or make a sound.

Others burst through the door then, two of them spraying the room with automatic weapons fire. The rounds snapped through the air and slammed into the walls, riddling them and filling the room with dust and dirt.

Without having to say a word or give an order, more men entered into the room and then through it. Salinas stepped to the dead men, all of them local soldiers. Two had been killed by the grenades which had shredded their uniforms and their bodies, turning them into bloodied hunks of dead meat. Another had been shot four or five times. Part of his head had been blown away, leaving a hole that showed the grey green slime of his jellied brain. The last man lay on his back, a peaceful look on his face but with two bullet holes in his chest. Blood was pooling around him.

Two of Salinas's men moved in and took weapons from the dead. They checked the pockets, stealing the wallets and then the rings and watches and anything else that might have value. Salinas ignored that, figuring that the dead had no need of their valuables anymore.

He headed through the far door, and heard more firing from above him. There was a groan and then a shout. Shooting erupted, the rounds smashing into the walls. The stairwell was thick with dust and cordite.

"Upstairs," shouted Salinas.

Two men sprinted around him. Salinas followed them, taking the stairs two at a time. He stopped on a landing, listened as the firing died. He moved again, finding the body of one of his men. He crouched near it and reached for the throat, finding no pulse.

His men were on either side of the door that led into the main part of the building. They were standing there, holding their weapons at port arms, waiting for orders.

Salinas moved to them and asked, "What's going on?"

"Barricaded man, maybe two. Firing everytime we open the door."

Salinas nodded and shouted down the stairs, "Get me an RPG up here. Now!"

A moment later a soldier holding the weapon appeared. He looked at the body and then at his commander.

"When we open the door, you fire at the first target you see."

"Yes, sir."

"Ready?"

The grenadier nodded and one of the men reached for the door handle. The grenadier crouched, his weapon up on his shoulder, his thumb on the trigger.

"Go," said Salinas.

The door was whipped open. The grenadier saw a desk turned on its side, the top facing him. He aimed and fired just as the enemy popped up, shooting his AK. The bullets stitched the grenadier across the chest, driving him back, into the railing. He hit it and bounced forward, falling face down.

As he did, the men slammed the door. There was an explosion from the other side of it that shook it. Smoke boiled up, from under the crack between the bottom of the door and the floor.

"Go!" shouted Salinas again.

One of the men grabbed the knob and hauled it open. Smoke from a dozen small fired rolled out, obscuring everything in the stairwell. The other soldier leaped in, followed by Salinas and then the last man. They spread out, but the sniper lay behind the desk, dead.

The grenade had hit the center of the desk and blown through it. The round hit the man and ripped him in half, spilling his intestines, stomach and liver onto the blood soaked floor. Salinas looked at the body and then ran passed it.

From elsewhere came the sound of more shooting. Muffled pops of single shots and the loud ringing of automatic weapons occasionally punctuated by grenades.

Salinas walked to the window and looked out on the concrete ramp that led from the building out to the airfield. There were four men lying dead on it and a small firefight on one corner. Quick flashes of fire from the muzzles of weapons. A fifth man fell and then a sixth, and Salinas saw his men rolling over the ramp like the incoming tide.

"Floor secure, Major."

"Then upstairs." He whirled and ran back to the door. He opened it, glanced at the dead grenadier and then ran on up. He came to a trapdoor in the floor above him and tried to open it. When it didn't budge, he rapped on it, yelling for whoever was hiding in the tower to open up or die.

When there was no response, Salinas stepped back, aimed, and fired five rounds into the door. "Open it or die."

There was a moment of silence and then the sound of a bolt being thrown. When the door opened, Salinas swarmed up the steps, his weapon held waist high. He burst into the tower, saw two men and a women backed against the radios and other equipment there, and looked out onto the whole airfield.

"What now, Major?" asked one of the men who had followed him up the stairs.

"Take these people outside and hold them under guard."

"Yes sir."

"You, out of here," barked the soldier.

The three people moved across the tower floor, their hands held over their heads. Awkwardly, they climbed down, disappearing from sight. As they did, Salinas sat down in the controller's chair and used a pair of binoculars he found there to survey the airfield. He could see the shapes of his soldiers as they moved around, securing the hangars and other buildings. They were running shadows, dodging right and left, sometimes firing short bursts that gave them the motion of figures in old black and white movies. There were a few small fires burning and a dozen bodies lying frozen on the ground. From a couple of positions came the flashing lights that told him those places had been secured.

Another of his soldiers appeared, sticking his head up, into the tower. "Field's secure. Radio men are ready."

"Bring them on up."

"Yes sir."

"How were the casualties?"

The sergeant shrugged and said, "A little stiffer than anticipated. Twelve dead so far and fourteen wounded. Two seriously."

"All right. Find Captain Allende and have him report to me here and have Captain Auturo consolidate our holdings and prepare for the counter-attack."

"Do you still expect one?"

"Of course. Of all the objectives, this is the most important. Without it, they can't easily bring in supplies and other soldiers. They'll attempt to take the airfield back first."

"Yes sir." The sergeant turned to go.

"I want to be kept informed on the casualties. Have the surgeon report to me here as soon as it is safe for him to do so. And have him arrange transport for the wounded, if they need to be taken to Los Banos."

"Yes sir."

The sergeant disappeared and Salinas looked out to the airfield. There were no more signs of the attack. They had taken the field easily, but then a surprise attack always met with early success. It was how strong, how well organized, and how determined the enemy was that decided who won or who lost the battle. Given the state of the military on Grande Terre de la Desirade, they probably would not be able to mount much of a counter-attack.

Salinas rocked back in the chair, locked his hands behind his head and put his feet up. The only thing missing was a fine Cuban cigar and he'd be able to get that in the morning when the re-supply plane landed.

# 3

"Why in the hell are we going to do a stupid thing like that?" demanded the Captain who had been in the club.

Owens looked at him, stared at him, trying to force him to back down, but it was a wasted effort. Neither man would bend to the other.

Finally Owens said, "Captain Banse, the reason for that should be obvious. There is an airport on the island and with just a little effort, the runways can be lengthened to handle the biggest jets. There are port facilities on the sheltered bay and a very little dredging could turn them into first class."

"Which still doesn't answer the question," said Banse.

Owens wiped a hand across his forehead and then scratched an eye. He grinned then and said, "Maybe invade was too harsh a word. An invasion implies that we have territorial demands and that once the fighting is over, we plan to retain possession of the real estate. That simply is not the case here." He glanced to the right. "Commander Marcel?"

Again Marcel moved to the maps. "As most of you know, there is a communist presence on Cuba."

Banse laughed outright. Tynan smiled and a couple of others nodded quietly. One of the women said, "Presence is putting it lightly."

"The problem there," said Marcel, "is that Castro is a strong force. He rules with an iron hand, and although he accepts aid, both economic and military, from the Soviet Union, he is not a puppet to their whims. He can and does say no to them."

"Fine," said Banse. "Tell us something we don't already know."

"What you don't know," said Marcel, "what you haven't read in *Time* or *Newsweek*, is that the Soviets have found another sphere of influence in the Caribbean."

"There's a Soviet presence there? On this Land of Desire?" asked Banse, surprised.

Marcel stepped back and rubbed his chin. "Well, that's not exactly right. There are hints of it and the Cubans have been sending technicians there by the boatload. The Cubans assist the Soviets to gain their island foothold and everyone's happy except old Uncle Sam."

Banse shook his head and said, "I don't think that receiving aid from the Cubans and the Russians is a sufficient reason for invading."

"No," agreed Owens, taking over for Marcel, "but we believe things are about to escalate. When they do, we have to be ready to move."

"Escalate how?" asked Tynan.

Marcel looked at Owens who nodded. Marcel then picked up a file folder that had a big red SECRET stamped at the top and the bottom. Opening it, he said, "Word is that the Cubans are mobilizing to move on the island. A full scale assault involving an airborne battalion to take and hold key points such as the airport, government radio stations and the presidential palace. A seaborne assault force of an infantry regiment and two battalions of construction workers boarded ships which have yet to leave port. The speculation from Central Intelligence is that these will be the troops used to subdue the local military and police and to make the changes to the airport and the seaport that we discussed."

"Christ," said Banse. "That's almost open warfare."

"Done quickly, it could look like a coup. One, two days without contact and the next thing we know, the President of Desirade is asking the Russians for aid."

Tynan shook his head and said, "I'm not sure that I should be here. This isn't something that falls into my expertise."

"Be patient, Lieutenant," said Owens. "We might not need you, but if we do, we want someone who is briefed on the situation, able to act quickly."

"Yes sir."

Marcel flipped one sheet of paper over and said, "We suspect an overt move sometime in the next seventy-two to ninety-six hours and we want to be ready to move within six hours of hearing about it."

There was a knock at the door and a sailor stuck his head in. He looked first at Owens and then to Marcel. When the commander nodded, the sailor entered and handed a note to Marcel. As the sailor retreated, Marcel said, "Oh Christ," and handed it to Owens.

He scanned it quickly and said, "Gentlemen. And ladies. Our two or three days of planning time has just evaporated. Reports are that the local radio station is off the air and the airport is diverting the air traffic other islands."

"Oh shit," said Banse.

Owens nodded and said, "I think that sizes it up pretty well. Now, we've got a lot of work to do quickly."

Kehoe stood with her shoulder touching Godwin. She reached down, found his hand and gripped it tightly. "What the hell is going on?"

Godwin shook his head. "I don't know. It looks a little strange."

"Strange hell," said a masculine voice. "It's a damned coup, that's what it is."

They watched as the parachutists hit the ground, most of them disappearing into the shadows. There were shapes running, flashes of light and then gunfire. The first burst caught them by surprise, none of them knowing what it was. But then one of the soldiers, either the Cuban attackers or the local defenders fired tracers and everyone knew what those were. They dived for cover behind the low stone wall on the roof.

"Shit," said Godwin. He peeked over the wall, saw an explosion on the airfield and watched flames spread in a gasoline fire, looking like a flaming river.

"What are we going to do?" asked Kehoe, her voice high and tight. She was kissing the rooftop, afraid to move or to even look up.

"You should have gotten out of here last week," said Godwin. "Hell, I should have gotten out of here last week, when I had the chance."

There was a distant rattle of gunfire. Bursts of it and then silence. The noise of the city had dropped away as if everyone in the place was holding his breath, waiting for the next move. Music had died, the radio was gone and the traffic had disappeared. Everyone knew that something was happening and to hit the streets to learn about it could be fatal.

"What are we going to do?" demanded Kehoe, her face still pressed against the rooftop.

Godwin risked another look and saw that more of the airfield was burning. Small fires at the edges of buildings. Nothing that looked as if it would spread.

"The safest thing is for us to lock the doors and then wait for someone to come and get us. The American embassy knows that we're here. Washington knows that there are a lot of American students here. We just wait for someone to come and get us."

One of the others said, "Let's get back inside."

Godwin nodded, realized that no one could see that now that the lantern had been extinguished. One of the boys got up and ran toward the door, hunched over like a combat soldier storming the beaches at Iwo Jima.

"On come, Vicki." He stood and half ran to the door. He stopped and waited for her and then together, they scrambled down the stairs.

"Now what?" she asked.

Godwin wasn't sure. He glanced down the hallway, which was dark and hot and smelled of stale beer and old vomit. He wiped the sweat from his face and rubbed it on his cut-offs.

"I don't know. There's nothing we can do until morning anyway. Nothing will happen until then."

"Maybe we should try to call someone," said Kehoe.

"Who?"

She shrugged. "I don't know. The embassy? The school administration? I don't know."

"I would think," said Godwin, "that our best move is to stay put, in here, and wait. No one's going to bother us."

But as he said it, an image flashed in his mind. The local residents, hating the rich Americans living in comfort at the university while they struggled endlessly to live one day to the next. The only thing holding them in check was the threat of the local police who would drag them off and lose them in the swamps if anything happened to the students. Police protection might be gone now. It might be time to hole up.

"Not until morning," he said to himself.

"What?"

"Nothing. Nothing we can do until morning."

Kehoe held onto his hand. "Listen," she said, her voice embarrassed, "I don't want to spend tonight alone."

"That's no problem," said Godwin.

"I'm not asking you to sleep with me, just stay with me. You understand the difference."

"Of course."

"Okay, then." She pulled him down the hall and into her room. She shut the door and then turned to the window. Through it, they could see the airfield, the fires a little bigger now. Shapes were moving, some of them fighting the fires, others seeming to guard the firefighters. Kehoe moved to the window and looked out it.

"We should never have come here," she said.

"Maybe not, but we're here now."

She dropped to the floor and sat crossed legged there. She wiped the sweat from her face and rubbed it on her blouse. Pulling the wet material away from her chest, she blew down it as if it would cool her.

Godwin sat down beside her. "Listen. Nothing's going to happen tonight because no one knows what's going on. We're as safe here tonight as if we were home. Tomorrow might be interesting, but right now we've nothing to worry about."

She moved closer to him and took his hand again. It seemed she was trying to draw strength from him. "You're sure?"

"Of course."

From the control tower, Salinas watched everything that was going on the airfield below him. His troops rounded up the guards who still lived and herded them into one corner of a hangar, making them sit on the floor. A few of the men were using the airport equipment to fight the fires, putting them out quickly, and the rest were patrolling the grounds to keep the civilians out and to search for attempts by the locals to take the airfield back.

Allende, who had reported and then been dispatched, returned. He sat down in a chair opposite of Salinas. His face was sweaty and dirt streaked. The camouflage paint he had worn for the assault had been wiped away.

"Fires are all under control and we've located the back up generator. I have the engineer working to get it started. We should have power in a few minutes."

"Good. How many prisoners do we have?"

"Near two hundred. They're all fairly docile now that we've their weapons."

"You have the anti-aircraft batteries erected?"

"Yes sir. One battery at each end of the runways, and one gun set up on the center of the field. We'll strengthen all that once the ships arrive."

"Good," said Salinas nodding. He took off his helmet and dropped it to the floor. He unbuckled his pistol belt and took off the weapon, setting it on the console near his hand. Without that to bind him, he felt better, more comfortable. Now all he needed was that cigar and a bottle of wine.

"I've also some of my men checking out the equipment

here, getting it ready for us. Airport should be fully opera-
tional by tomorrow. We can bring our transports as soon as
we get some power."

It was almost as if his words were magic. There was a
buzzing in the control tower and then the lights around
them flickered into brilliance, faded, and then came on
again, remaining steady. Salinas found a dimmer and
turned them down. The radio popped and crackled with
static, and the runway and taxiway lights all burst on, outlining the airfield for the pilots.

"Let's get one of our controllers up here and have him
bring in the transports."

"Yes sir. And I'll use the radio to coordinate tomorrow's
landings as well."

"Good."

Allende left the control tower. A moment later a sergeant carrying his own radio equipment entered. He set up
the radio on a ledge around the inside of the tower. He
leaned the antenna against the glass and turned on the portable radio. There was a single burst of static and he turned
the gain knob to eliminate it.

"Can't you use the equipment here?" asked Salinas.

"Oh, yes sir. I just wanted to get this set up as a back up
in case we lose the power again."

The sergeant then sat down at the console, flipped a few
switches, dialed the radios and listened to the tuning
squeals as the radios cycled. He checked it all again, made
sure that he had the right frequency and then rocked back.
That done, he picked up the mike, made a single call and
was answered by the pilot of the lead transport.

"Should I bring them in?"

Salinas stood and studied the airfield. The fires were
out, his men were in control, and the lights were now on.

The various units and teams had reported in, claiming they held the whole field. No resistance was being reported and the firing was far off the airport and inside the city. There was no reason not to let the transports land.

"Go ahead and give them the order."

"Yes sir."

Salinas sat down again and thought to himself, "It was easier than I thought it would be."

# 4

Owens didn't hesitate when he heard the news. He looked at Tynan and said, "How fast can you get a team together?"

"To do what?" asked Tynan.

"To move on the airport and recapture it. Secure the various facilities and eliminate the armed presence."

"You're talking about six, eight men sneaking in to eliminate what, three, four thousand guys. Six of us in an act of war ordered by a captain."

Owens rocked back and stared up at the ceiling. To the people assembled there, he said, "Before we initiate any activity, we'd have clearance from the White House, the State Department and the Pentagon."

"Fine, Captain," said Tynan, "but what you're talking about is not a mission that fits into the framework of our operations. Pathfinding, clearing mine fields, eliminating a command structure, sneak and peek operations, certainly. Taking on three battalions of infantry, no. Kill the officers in those battalions, maybe."

Banse interrupted. "I think we're getting ahead of ourselves here. There is nothing we can do until official policy is determined by the President."

"Not true," said Owens. "We can formulate plans and put the wheels in motion so that we've eliminated the preliminary steps when the balloon does go up."

He waited and when no one said a word, he turned toward Tynan. "Now, Lieutenant, I would imagine that your role, if we have an operation, will be along the lines outlined by you. In and out. Maybe a pathfinder mission. Maybe something to slow the enemy response to our appearance. Something to inhibit them. Tell me what you need."

Tynan sat back, closed his eyes and tried to think. At the very least, transport. Parachute into the airfield, or if close enough to the ocean, off a sub into the water and then across the dry land. Depending on the target, take out the electrical power to the airfield or set up to snipe at the officers. A mission in to disrupt the power and the reinforcements made some sense. A quick operation to capture the airfield would work. The assassinations idea didn't have enough time. He'd have to put together a team and there'd be no time to study the targets. They'd have to be killed the night they hit the island and there were too many opportunities to get fucked up.

"First thing I need," said Tynan, "is the definition of my mission. Without that, I haven't a clue as to what I'm going to need."

Owens looked at Marcel and the back at the others. "My assumption is that the President is going to want us to remove the Cuban influence on the island. Now, first will be diplomatic suggestions that Cuban forces not be deployed. Deals will be made, threats will be exchanged and in the end, force will be needed to convince the Cubans of our resolve."

Tynan laughed. "With every college campus aflame, with congress now opposing the war in Vietnam, it's going to be damned hard to convince Castro and the Russians that we're serious about keeping them out. Empty threats."

Marcel nodded. "The Lieutenant has a point, Captain. We won't be able to bluff it out."

"A task force in the Caribbean . . ." said Owens.

"No," said Banse. "I must concur. They will be no bluffs now. We'll have to use force."

Owens nodded and said, "The simplest move is to take out the military leaders on the island." He turned and stared right at Tynan. "You have a problem with that?"

"Not if the orders are written and from the appropriate authorities. I'll need dossiers on the targets, pictures of them and anything else available. I'll need locations on the island because we can't be expected to search for the targets too. And I'd need forty-eight hours on the island before anyone could expect us to even begin."

"That's asking a great deal," said Owens.

"And that hasn't even provided us with weapons, transportation to and rescue from the island. It hasn't given me the size of the team, or the number of targets were expected to hit."

"Captain Banse can get you to the island."

"Not for three days, if we left tonight," he said.

"Jillian can give you the data you need."

"Not unless you can identify the units that are involved in the coup. Then, for the lower ranking officers, we probably have nothing available. Our files don't extend down to the colonels and major unless there is something significant about the man," she said. "And the odds of having anything on the locals is remote. The president of the island, yes. The military and police officials? Not likely."

Owens fell silent. He looked around the room and then at the notes in front of him. "You all seem reluctant to participate in this activity."

Tynan waited for the others and when no one spoke, he said, "It's not a reluctance to participate in this. It's a reluctance to go off half-cocked. We need specific information. We can't just throw a mission together with no planning and expect it to work."

"All right, Lieutenant. I want you to get together with Jillian and see what you can come up with for an assassination mission. I want a time table that can be followed, a list of supplies you'll need and people you'll want with you. That specific enough?"

"Yes sir," said Tynan. "I will also need intell reports on the island." He glanced at Marcel. "More detail than you gave us in the preliminary."

"Jillian has access to all that, Lieutenant. Now, when could you hit the field?"

Tynan sat quietly and stared at the wall. "Twenty-four hours, but that's pushing it. A week would be better."

"Assume you have the twenty-four," said Owens, "and pray you get the week."

"Aye aye, sir."

"If there is nothing else you need," said Owens, "I would suggest you get to work. I'll expect a progress report by noon tomorrow."

Tynan stood up and repeated, "Aye aye, sir."

He moved to the door and then stopped, waiting for the woman who was assigned to work with him. She stood, closed up the notepad in front of her, folded it under her arm and then joined him at the door.

She was a tall, slender woman with short blond hair and brown eyes. Her face was long and thin with a pointed chin, small, button nose and eyebrows so light and fine that they were nearly invisible. She wore a white blouse and a black, pleated skirt.

"You ready?" she asked.

Tynan opened the door and as she stepped through, she said, "You have a car?"

"Upstairs and waiting."

"Good, we'll take it over to my office and begin our work there."

As they reached the stairs, Tynan said, "Excuse me, but I don't really know who you are."

She stopped, and turned to face him. Holding out a hand, she said, "I'm Jillian Carter. I'm the local spook."

"I didn't know that we had a local spook assigned here," said Tynan.

Starting up the stairs, she laughed, "I'm not CIA if that's what you mean. I'm in Air Force intelligence."

"Ah," said Tynan. Then looked at her again. "Air Force and not Naval."

"Air Force. I'm assigned to the airlifting wing based here. We have our own needs."

"Then why are you and not Naval Intelligence in on this?" asked Tynan.

"I think because of the data that I have in my files," she said. She shrugged. "I really don't know why I was told to be here."

They reached the ground floor and walked down the hallway to where the sailor at the table waited. Both signed out and then Tynan opened the door for her. They stepped out into a wet world where there was no longer any rain. Lights from the streetlamps and cars reflected from the puddles created by the thunderstorm. The humidity hung in the air, visible. A haze that created circles of color around the lights.

Tynan pointed to the car and they walked toward it. Strong, apparently watching in the rearview mirror, leaped from the driver's side and opened the rear doors. Tynan let

Carter enter, trying not to look as her skirt rode up her thighs.

"Where to, Lieutenant?" asked Strong.

Tynan got into the back and said, "Ms. Carter?"

"Jillian, please." She ducked down slightly so that she could look at the driver. "You know where building seven ten is?"

"Of course."

"Take us over there."

Strong closed the door and then climbed into the driver's seat. She started the engine, slipped it into gear and then pulled out. There was almost no traffic on the base now that it was after midnight.

Carter lowered her voice and asked, "How'd you get roped into this thing?"

"I don't know," said Tynan. "I was on temporary duty here. I was minding my own business at the club when I was told that a driver would come from me." He stopped and looked at her. The red lipstick she wore was smudged slightly. He pulled her eyes away and asked, "Owens always this volatile?"

"He tends to think in terms of grand global strategy which defines my role here. He browbeat some other captain and had me attached to his staff for some kind of feasibility study that required specialized information. This alert is a God-send to him."

They rode in silence and then stopped outside a rambling, two story brick building. There were lights on outside it, illuminating the rain wet parking lot. There were only a few cars in it and only a couple of lights on inside the building. Most of the windows were dark.

Strong turned and looked over the back of the seat. "You going to need me anymore tonight?"

Carter said, "I've got a car here if we need it."

"I guess you can go," said Tynan.

"What about tomorrow?" she asked.

"I'll call the motor pool if I need anyone tomorrow," said Tynan.

"Yes sir. Good night, sir." Then, as an afterthought added, "Oh, and you too, ma'am."

Tynan opened the door and got out. Carter followed, closed it and immediately, the car took off.

"I'm afraid I made your girlfriend mad."

"Just met her tonight. Nice girl," said Tynan.

Carter ignored that and walked up the steps to the front door. She pushed it opened and then led Tynan down a darkened hallway to her office. Using a key she took from the pocket of her skirt, she unlocked the door. Opening it, she reached inside for the light switch.

The office wasn't much. There was a single desk, battleship grey, old and beat up. There was a phone on the corner of it, a blotter in the center and a wheeled chair. Along one wall were file cabinets, two of them normal letter files, and one a heavy duty model with a combination lock on it. Opposite them was a table littered with the current news magazines, newspapers, and non-fiction books.

Carter threw her keys on the desk, set her notepad down, and said, "Have a seat."

Tynan took the visitor's chair and waited. Carter opened her safe, pulled out a manual and handed it to him. "This will give you everything you want to know about Grande Terre as of six months ago. It's only three months old so the info is current as of last May."

"Thanks."

Carter closed the door to the office and then sat down at her desk. She reached from the phone, dialed and then said, "I'll be here for the next six or eight hours. We may need some specific intelligence hand carried to us." She waited, nodded and added, "Of course."

Tynan scanned the information in the CIA publication. It told him nothing that he hadn't heard at the briefing. There was a map of the island showing the capital city, the location of the airport and the system of roads on the island. He finished, closed the book and said, "I'm through."

Carter spun around to face him. "As soon as we determine what we need, I can get it up here. Our problem is that I don't have the facilities to store top secret material."

Tynan nodded. He looked at his watch. "I can't think of what I should be doing without knowing what Owens is going to want. If it's sabotage, I'll need one team, if it's assassination, another, and pathfinding, he could use the Army's rangers. He doesn't need me."

"He seems to think that it's going to be assassination," said Carter.

"All right," said Tynan. "I want a legal pad to list the names of the men I'd want. Then, I'll want that information you said you could get."

"As soon as the units are identified," she said.

Tynan laughed. "We're spinning our wheels here."

"Owens said that he wants a report by noon."

Tynan shrugged. "I could give it to him now. We're working, but without a little more information, there isn't much to be done. I'd be wasting my time if I tried to come up with anything now."

Carter spun again and leaned her elbows on the desk. Staring at the phone, she said, "We should be doing something."

"Nope," said Tynan. "Not without some kind of direction. What we should do is catch some sleep, eat breakfast and return here about nine. Then, if the situation has soli-

dified, I can throw together something that will make
Owens happy."

"That fast?"

Tynan grinned. "Well, any mission he wants is a fairly
standard operation. We just need to plug in the variables
and it looks good." He stopped talking and said, "Don't
tell anyone that I told you that."

"Your secret is safe with me. I'm trained in keeping
secrets."

"Then if you'll give me a lift over to the VOQ . . ."

Carter stood up and stuffed the CIA manual back into
the safe, locking it. "I'm not comfortable with this," she
said.

"Jillian, there's nothing for us to do tonight. Sitting here
worrying about it is going to do us no good."

Grabbing her keys, she said, "I guess you're right."

"If it'll make you happy, I'll meet you at five for breakfast and we can come back here."

"Make it six and you've got a deal."

"Done," he said.

They left the office together, with Carter stopping long
enough to lock the door. She didn't turn off the light,
wanting anyone who drove by to think that she was still
there. A minor deception, but part of the political games
that everyone played on all military bases.

They drove in silence to the VOQ. When she stopped
near the front, she asked, "You want me to call for you?"

"If you don't mind."

"Then I'll see you tomorrow."

"Tomorrow," said Tynan.

She dropped the car into gear and drove off. As the
taillights flashed, Tynan shook his head and asked, "How
do I get into these messes?"

# 5

It was a long, hot night, the quiet split with occasional shots and bursts of machine gun fire. The lights flickered once, stayed on for two or three minutes and then went out. The fans that had remained plugged in whirled, blowing around the hot air, and then died as the power failed again.

Godwin couldn't sleep. It was too hot, sometimes too noisy, and even though he'd told Kehoe not to worry, he was frightened. The shooting, the failure of the power, and the paratroopers he had seen told him that something was happening. He spent part of the time at the window, watching everything that he could see below him.

And what scared him the most was that there wasn't that much to watch. A few shadows running down the street, an armored personnel carrier that rumbled by, and no traffic. The government of the island was changing hands and when that happened, people poured into the streets to loot and kill.

Kehoe slept fitfully, tossing and turning, and sitting up suddenly when there was gunfire. Always she asked the same question, "What was that?"

"Nothing," said Godwin.

"I heard shooting."

"Miles away. Go back to sleep."

As the sun came up, Godwin was standing in the window, looking out at the city. There was smoke on the horizon. Thick black smoke that drifted slowly to the east. There was smoke to the south. Several columns of it, not as black or as thick.

But more importantly, there was no traffic on the roads. Normally the city hadn't had many cars or trucks or buses, but by dawn they were out as the people moved from their houses to work or the marketplace. Now the streets were vacant.

"What's happening?" asked Kehoe.

Godwin turned and looked at her. The light blouse she was wearing was soaked with sweat, becoming almost transparent. It was obvious that she was not wearing a bra and Godwin tried to keep from staring at her.

"Nothing," he said.

"That's good."

"No," he said, shaking his head. "I mean nothing at all. There are no people on the streets. No cars or buses or anything."

"What are we going to do?"

Godwin rubbed his face and said, "I think that maybe it's time for us to get out of here and to the embassy. I don't like what I'm seeing."

Kehoe got up and moved to the window, looking down at the streets and the gardens surrounding the university. There were a few students on the grounds, but not many of them. There were no people on the streets.

"I don't like this," she said.

"Neither do I."

\* \* \*

Salinas spent the night in the control tower, watching as the transports landed, spit out the men and equipment and then lifted off again. Once the aircraft was clear, the men and equipment were moved, hurriedly, to one of the hangers where it and they were checked, cross-checked, and then told what to do or where to store it. The idea was to give satellite imagery nothing to look at when the spy satellites flew over.

As each group arrived, one of the officers would report to Salinas in the tower. He'd take their report and then dismiss them. That was, until Lieutenant Alverez appeared.

"Special dispatch," he said, handing a folder over to Salinas.

Salinas took the folder and spun around so that his back was to Alverez. He turned on a small lamp over the console and placed the folder in the pool of brightness. After reading the one page memo quickly, he spun around to face the lieutenant.

"You know the contents of this directive?"

"Yes sir."

"And were you given any verbal instructions that concern it?"

"No sir. Just that you are to act upon it at your discretion, remembering that we want to do nothing to involve the United States or the Organization of American States in our activities here."

Salinas glanced at the document and waved it like a banner. "This tells me nothing."

"Yes sir," agreed Alverez.

"All right," said Salinas. He leaned forward and shouted down the stairs, "Guerruro, get up here."

The sergeant appeared and said, "Yes sir."

"I want a platoon of men ready to move in one hour.

Good, steady men, one officer and we'll use vehicles."

Guerruro nodded and retreated down the stairs. Alverez watched him go and then asked, "What are you planning to do?"

"We don't want anything to happen to the students. I'm going to deploy a platoon of men around the university to protect them, of course."

"Such a move might be misinterpreted."

Salinas shrugged. "Leaving them alone might prove to be even more dangerous."

He fell silent and watched the activities on the field for a moment. Then he turned back to Alverez. "You might have a point there. I'll accompany the troops to the university and explain the situation so there won't be any mistakes."

When the last of the scheduled transports had landed and taken off, Salinas rocked back in his chair, looking like a man who had put in an eight hour shift as an air traffic controller. His fatigue uniform was sweatsoaked. His jet black hair hung down over his forehead and there were dark circles under his eyes. Wiping at the seat with one hand, he stood up.

"Allende, you'll have control here. Keep the radio on and listen for more of our planes. Guerruro downstairs can serve as your runner."

"Yes sir. And you'll be?"

"With the platoon heading over to the university. We'll maintain radio contact. No messages unless important."

"Yes sir."

Salinas, feeling suddenly tired, climbed down from the tower and then to the steps that would take him down to the ground floor. As he descended, he noticed that some of the debris caused by the attack had been cleaned up already. There was a smear of blood where the grenadier had been killed and the door leading to the second floor was filled with holes. On the ground floor, he could see where that fight had taken place. In the corner of the large room were a number of sheet draped corpses. Here the debris was still scattered.

He walked out and realized that the air still hung heavy with humidity. Wisps of light fog surrounded the plants. Two of his men walked toward him and when he shook his head, they turned, returning to their duty.

Salinas found Alverez standing outside a hangar smoking a cigarette and watching the sunrise. "Are you going with us?" asked Salinas.

"If you don't mind, Major."

"Not at all."

Alverez flipped away his cigarette and turned. Salinas opened the door and found two armored personnel carriers and forty men waiting. The men were all wearing fatigues, carried AK-47s and were wearing pistol belts holding canteens, ammo pouches and first aid kits.

"Lieutenant Batiste, reporting, sir."

"Your men are ready?"

"At your command, Major."

Salinas nodded and said, "Have them load up. I want a jeep for the lead vehicle. This is to be a nice, quiet, little adventure. No one shoots."

"Yes sir."

A moment later a jeep pulled up and Salinas climbed into the passenger's seat. Batiste hopped into the back as the rest of his men scattered, entering the armored personnel carriers. Their engines roared to lift, belching clouds of diesel smoke. As that happened, the huge hangar door began to open, telescoping into itself so that the vehicles could drive out.

Batiste had a street map out and was looking at it as they roared through the broken down chain-link fence that surrounded the airport. They drove down a palm lined street that had white, one story buildings set back, away from the curb, insulated by green lawns and tropical plantings. Wrought iron fences with pointed tips that masked as decorations kept the locals away from the fine houses.

Within a block or two all that changed. There were buildings up against the curb with almost no sidewalk between them and the street. Old buildings, some with broken glass covered by plywood and corrugated tin roofs. The streets narrowed and the palms were gone.

But then another turn brought them to a park. Palms and coconut trees and broadleafed bushes covered with brightly colored flowers in oranges and yellows. And beyond that was the campus of the university.

Salinas saw the three, four and five story structures made of golden stone, looking like modern office and apartment buildings in any city in the world. A status symbol of sorts. One that was unavailable to the local population.

As they moved along the streets, Salinas saw some of his soldiers stationed on street corners. There were a few roadblocks erected to turn traffic from the country around. No one was allowed in or out of the city.

They came to the university and stopped. Salinas climbed out of the jeep and stood there, looking up at the windows of the building. The armored personnel carriers pulled up behind him and the men leaped out, forming a line in the street.

"Lieutenant, spread your men out and have them round up the students." He glanced at the right and then shrugged. "There must be a gym or an auditorium somewhere. Take them all there. Tell them that there is nothing to worry about and we're doing this for their own protection."

"Yes sir."

"Oh, and tear down all the phone lines that you can find. We'll want to limit their communications with the outside world until we're ready for it."

"Yes sir." Batiste spun, shouting orders. The men began to filter onto the campus.

"Now," whispered Salinas to himself, "if everyone remains calm, we'll be in good shape."

"Oh shit," yelled Godwin.

"What!?"

"Soldiers. Soldiers on the campus." He ducked down, peeking out the window.

Kehoe dropped to the floor like she'd been shot. "What are we going to do?"

"I don't know," said Godwin. He wiped at his face, suddenly slick with sweat that hadn't been caused by the humidity. "Let me think."

A whistle sounded and there was a shout. Godwin risked another look out the window. Two soldiers were chasing a man across the campus. A young, bearded man who had wanted to escape American police on an American campus by coming to a tropical island.

"They're arresting us," said Godwin.

"What are we going to do?" Kehoe's voice had risen an octave with fright.

"I don't know," he snapped. He got up and walked to the door and looked into the hall. No one was there. The other students were hiding in their rooms, or in the rooms of their fellow students.

He turned and glanced at Kehoe. "We need to get out of here. Hide somewhere."

From outside there was a shout. A command. They couldn't understand the words, but the tone was clear. The soldiers were giving orders to all the civilians that they found.

Kehoe moved to the closet and pulled out a pair of blue jeans. She stripped the shorts she had been wearing, ignoring Godwin as she did, and pulled on the jeans. She found a clean cotton shirt and replaced the sweat soaked blouse she had been wearing.

"I'm ready."

"Okay," said Godwin. "Okay. What we need is a place with a lock on the door, like a store room and not a dorm room."

"How about the girl's john?"

"No good. They'd expect someone to hide there." Godwin moved to the door and searched the hallway again. He waved at her. "Come on."

They hurried down the hallway, stopping long enough for Godwin to grab a shirt. They reached the end of the corridor and found a small storeroom. Godwin ripped open the door, saw that it was jammed with buckets, mops and cleaning supplies. There was a dirty sink on the far wall that would provide them with water if they needed some during the wait. There was the odor of cleaning fluid and wax filling the air.

"In here," said Godwin.

"For how long?"

"I don't know. An hour or two. Until they search this floor we'll have to stay hidden. We'll be able to hear them and know when they've finished."

Kehoe entered it, pushed a bucket to the side and then dusted her hands off. "It smells in here."

Godwin pushed in after her and closed the door. It was suddenly pitch black. He opened it a crack and shoved some of the material to the side, out of his way. As he sat down, he looked up and said, "You'd better get comfortable." He pulled a bucket over and leaned an elbow on it.

Without a word, Kehoe sat down. When she did, Godwin reached up to close the door and said, "We're going to have to be quiet now."

"I know."

"It'll only be for an hour," he said, and wished that he could convince himself of that.

# 6

Tynan was standing outside the VOQ when Carter drove up. She flashed her lights in recognition and then leaned across the front seat to open the passenger's side door.

As he climbed in, Tynan said, "I thought it would be cooler after the rain."

"Nope. Just makes it muggy." She spun the wheel and drove out of the parking lot. "You have a preference for breakfast?"

"Just some place where I can get a couple of eggs and some pancakes."

"How about steak and eggs?"

"That'd be perfect." He leaned forward and switched on the radio. "You mind if I look for the news?"

She slowed, stopped for a light and then accelerated again. "Go right ahead."

Tynan listened to snatches of music, rock and roll, country, and classical. He found a commercial, waited and then heard a preacher telling all who listened that the Lord knew what they were doing. He kept going, finally finding a weather report and hoping it was the lead into the news.

The announcer came on a few moments later with the d news. He talked about the war in Vietnam and student protests on several campuses. The Paris Peace talks were not going well with both sides suggesting that the other was not negotiating in good faith.

Then he talked about the sudden news blackout from the tiny island nation of Grande Terre. Government controlled radio talked about shooting at the airport before it went off the air. He promised to report more information as soon as it was available from the network.

"Usually the newsies have the information just as fast as we get it," said Carter.

"You get anything new since last night?"

"Probably," she said. She hit the blinker and pulled into the parking lot of a restaurant. She parked, turned off the engine and faced him.

"You didn't check?"

"No. I left the apartment and drove straight over to the VOQ."

Tynan rubbed his face. "I kind of wish you'd checked the message traffic."

"We can go do that now or we can go eat and then check the traffic. Up to you."

"We're here. Let's eat. Thirty or forty minutes isn't going to make that much difference."

They got out of the car as they entered the restaurant, Tynan bought a morning paper. The headlines told of the Vietnam War and the peace talks and the latest in the exploration of space. There was local news about a killing in the Five Points area and the police had been involved in a high speed pursuit with the killer.

They found a booth and the waitress brought water and menus and then disappeared. Tynan scanned the paper and said, "Nothing about it. Oh, here's something." He was quiet for a minute and then said, "Not much. Someone speculating about a coup on a Caribbean island." He folded the paper and set it on the seat beside him.

"What's your plan today?" she asked.

Before he could answer, the waitress was back. Carter ordered an omelette and tomato juice. Tynan had a steak, rare, fried eggs, hash browns and orange juice.

When the waitress disappeared, Tynan considered the question. "I guess provide a plan for mission A and one for mission B with a list of equipment and people needed for each of the plans."

Carter looked around. There weren't many people in the restaurant this early. Two men in jeans and flannel shirts at a table, a man and a woman at another and three college-age boys at a third who were probably sailors eating good food rather than mess hall chow. There wasn't much noise, as if everyone was trying to wake up before a day at work.

"So," she said to Tynan, "tell me about yourself."

Tynan was caught off guard by the question. He reached for the water, took a drink and said, "Not that much to tell. I spent some time in college and then joined the Navy."

"What college?"

"University of Colorado."

"Then you must be a skier."

Tynan laughed. "You know, I grew up in Colorado, went to college there and don't ski. Friends ski. A lot of them, but I just never got around to it."

"Why?"

"Well, there's another damned good question. I suppose if anyone had asked, I would have gone skiing, but we just didn't get into that."

"I guess that's the way it is with everyone. You grow up in Washington and you don't see the Capitol Building or the Smithsonian, grow up in New York and you don't see the Statue of Liberty."

"Now, I have been to the mint in Denver." He grinned. "But I didn't live in Colorado when I took the tour."

The food arrived. The waitress set it out, hesitated and then asked, "Anything else?"

"We're fine."

As she walked away, Tynan asked, "What about you?"

"Born in Iowa, grew up in Iowa and went to college in Iowa." She laughed. "When the Air Force," she looked around and then whispered, "Air Force recruiter came promising world travel, how could I resist." Her voice reached a normal tone again. "Of course, I haven't had the chance at world travel, but I'm not in Iowa anymore."

"There something wrong with Iowa?"

She thought for a moment and said, "No, not really. People on the coast see it as some vast almost unpopulated wasteland filled with farmers who don't have indoor plumbing but it's not like that. Oh, the people are skeptical of some of the newest fads, but then, some of those fads are ridiculous. They measure the murder rate by the number in the whole state for a year and not in a city for a week. A quiet place where they don't care about driving a brand new car every year. No, nothing wrong with Iowa."

"The good thing about Colorado," said Tynan, "is that no one says anything bad about it except to ask why I'd leave."

"And why did you?"

"It was either join the Navy after college or find myself as cannon fodder in the Army. Not much of a choice."

They ate in silence for a few minutes and then Carter looked at her watch. "Morning message traffic should have cleared by now. Get the latest on everything."

"You suggesting that I should eat faster?"

"No, just that you were worried about the messages and we can pick them up now."

Tynan finished eating, drained his juice and said, "Let's go then."

On the way to Carter's office, they stopped at the message center. It was a cinderblock building that had a guard on the gate who recognized Carter and let her in. Tynan followed her and stood behind her as she pressed the button to alert those inside that she was there. A painted window behind a set of bars opened and the clerk nodded in recognition, and slid the panel down again.

"Be a couple of minutes," she said.

"I'm familiar with the drill."

The clerk returned, opened the window panel and slipped a clipboard through. He pointed to the top line and then handed her a package of messages. "Check the date-time group for each message and then sign for them."

She handed the messages to Tynan and he read off the numbers while she checked them off. Satisfied that she was getting everything she was signing for, she scribbled her name. After handing the clipboard back to the clerk, she turned.

"Let's go."

Tynan had been glancing at the classified documents. Now he stuffed them back into the envelope. Together they walked back to the car, nodding at the guard. Once in the car, Tynan opened the envelope again and began searching for a reference to Grande Terre.

The problem was that a coup in a foreign country that didn't bother Americans or threaten American interests wasn't important. Not with the war in Vietnam going, with clandestine searches for POWs being conducted, and with the Paris peace talks stumbling along.

As they approached the office, Carter asked, "You find anything?"

"Not yet."

She pulled into her parking space and glanced at the messages he was holding, reading them. Tynan handed her a bunch from the bottom of the stack. She refused them, saying, "We'll wait until we're inside."

Tynan put everything back into the manilla envelope a final time. They left the car and hurried up, into the building. They stopped at the door, but when she reached down to unlock it, it swung partially open. She glanced at him, the question on her face.

"If we were anywhere else," he said, "I'd figure there was something wrong."

Carter pushed it all the way open and saw Owens sitting in her chair, reading the unclassified reports sitting on her desk. He turned as they entered.

"Where in the hell have you two been?"

"Over to the message center to pick up the traffic so that our briefings will be up to date."

Owens nodded and said, "Nice try. I called last night and got no answer." He stared at Tynan. "I thought I had given you orders, Lieutenant."

"Yes sir," said Tynan. "Ms. Carter and I returned here, made some progress and then called it a night. We caught some sleep, some breakfast and picked up the messages."

Owens stared at him, his eyes boring into Tynan. "I hope you're not telling me that you spent the night together."

"I think I resent your implication, Captain," said Carter. "Not to mention that what I do on my time is my business and I don't need you to keep an eye on me."

Owens had not taken his eyes off Tynan. The lieutenant moved to the desk and dropped the message traffic on the top of it. He tried to think of something to say, but nothing seemed right.

"There something you want, Captain?" asked Carter.

"Take a look at the messages and tell me what you think."

Tynan opened the envelope again, took out the flimsy documents. Carter moved closer to him and looked over his shoulder.

"Got it," said Tynan.

There wasn't much to it. Reports by the local CIA operative who watched as the Soviet built AN-26 Curls landed at the airfield. He talked of fighting at the airport, the one radio station and of troops in Cuban uniforms surrounding the presidential palace.

"Not so much a coup as an invasion from Cuba."

"Bingo," said Owens.

"What's Washington have to say about this?" asked Carter.

"Well, if you two had remained here last night, you would have known what your jobs were and could have been here getting ready to move."

Tynan scanned the rest of the report and then handed it to Carter. As she read it, Tynan sat down in the visitor's chair. Owens waited quietly.

Carter finished and said, "Not much here."

Owens said, "There is another complication that isn't in the report." He stood up and moved away, toward the file cabinet and leaned on it. "There is a medical school not more than a mile or two from the airfield."

Carter was impatient. "So?"

"Many of the students are Americans. Couldn't get into good American schools so they headed down there for their medical degrees."

"And you're going to tell me that the Cubans have taken them hostage," said Tynan.

"We don't know," said Owens, "but there is a possibility

that they will, if they learn about them. The President has expressed concern about them and has asked if there is anything we can do."

"Why not have the people in the embassy there head out and pick them all up?" asked Carter.

Owens grinned. "There's the rub. First, we don't have a full embassy there. Just a small operation, two or three people who are charged with carrying our flag, maintaining our presence there and in the Caribbean."

"Still . . ."

"Nothing," said Owens. "They have shut down the operation and have been pulled out for their protection."

"So there is no one out there to take care of our citizens on Grande Terre."

Owens looked at Tynan and said, "Not until you get your men deployed. Your job now is to get to our students in San Antonio and get them the hell out."

Tynan was quiet for a moment and then said, "Terrific."

# 7

Tynan listened to the whole story as Owens had it, and then sat at the desk when he left. He read through the report on the Grande Terre military and realized that it meant nothing now because a Cuban wildcard had been thrown into the game. He sat back, looked at Carter who was sitting stiffly in the visitor's chair.

"What? What do you need?"

Tynan rubbed his face and said, "I need a good map of San Antonio. One that has the university on it and the airport and other landmarks. Main hotels, rivers, bridges, temples and parks."

"You don't want much do you?"

"You're telling me that you don't have that?"

She took a deep breath and pointed at the four drawer file cabinet that was her safe. "I am required, by regulation, to keep certain items, given the mission of the units on this base. I must have route threat assessments, Soviet military capabilities that are updated every six months, and I must have factbooks on weapons systems, capabilities of those weapons and ranging information. I must keep the daily messages and the weekly messages and the current intelligence updates. All must be logged in, stored according to regulations and then destroyed when out of date. The records of the destruction must be kept for two years."

"So you don't have maps of San Antonio or Grande Terre," said Tynan.

"Hell, I'm lucky the factbook had anything on it. I mean, who the hell heard of this place before yesterday."

Tynan rubbed a hand through his hair. "You're making this difficult."

"Not me. It's the volume of information available." She laughed. "No, it's the availability of information. I could fill this room with data. Tons of it that could answer every question that you could ask. The problem is, I never know what the question is going to be. You want to invade Cuba, I have plenty of information about it. You interested in South America. I have files on that. I have information on the major African countries and European countries and if you have any questions about North or South Vietnam, I have a file draw full of papers, reports and factbooks on them."

She shook her head. "But you want information on Grande Terre, other than the little bit in the factbook, you're just shit out of luck."

"I understand the problem," said Tynan.

"No, I don't think you do. I think you think you do, but you don't. There is too much information available. You have spies trying to get it and traitors trying to sell it. You have reporters who feel the world owes them the information. There are historians and anthropologists gathering more. There are economists and there are researchers. Information is stored in books and magazines and computers and organized by librarians and historians. You can order factbooks and news magazines and never have a chance to read it all."

"I understand."

"The only thing I can do," she said ignoring his comment, "is try to anticipate. But who could anticipate this little rinky-dink island?"

"So you have nothing about it?"

"Not any more than is in the factbook."

"Okay," said Tynan, "here's an idea. I used it once before. How about a travel agent? Maybe they'd have something on it for tourists. Wouldn't be the best but might do it."

"Yeah," she said, nodding. "I could call down to the library and see if they have anything down there."

"I don't like this Cuban thing," said Tynan. "You got an Order of Battle for them?"

"I can give you something, but I don't think it will identify the units deployed on this."

Tynan shrugged. "I would think that an Order of Battle for the United States would have the Eighty-second Airborne tagged as one of the first units to deploy and that would be a fairly good guess."

"Except that the Eighty-second is in Vietnam," she reminded him.

"Right. Except for that."

Tynan vacated her chair. Carter took it and picked up the phone, making a few calls. Tynan sat in the visitor's chair, a legal pad on his lap. Now that the mission was defined, he could make a few guesses about the team now. A simple rescue was far less complicated than the original concepts of assassinations and pathfinding.

He created a list of names, men he'd worked with before. A short list because they wouldn't be facing a large enemy force. A sneak in and get out operation that would avoid bloodshed if they caught a few breaks. The fewer men that he took with him, the more likely they could get in and out without having to fight the locals or the Cubans.

He worked quietly until Carter said, "I think I found what we need. You interested in a trip downtown?"

"If we can swing by Owens's office first. I want him, or someone at his end to begin getting these people together for me."

"That's no problem."

There was a lot of noise in the building. There were shouts and screams and the sounds of people running. Some of it was below them and some of it above them. There were pounding on the walls and the doors and protests by people forced from their rooms. And there were a few shots. Random noises that might have been warnings to those who watched.

Godwin sat with his back against the wall, his knees hiked up, glad that he hadn't bothered with changing. The tiny room was hot, and smelled of dirty wax and dust. The air didn't move and sweat soaked his body, running like miniature rivers down his flesh.

The only good thing was that his eyes had adjusted to the dimness of the light from under the crack of the door. It was a bright strip that gave the shapes in the closet some dimension.

Neither he nor Kehoe had talked since they had dodged into the closet. They'd made places to sit and then locked the door, hoping that the soldiers wouldn't force the lock.

He glanced over at Kehoe. Her hair was soaked, looking like she'd just stepped from the shower. After only thirty minutes, she'd unbuttoned her blouse, trying to cool off, but it was impossible in the confined space. She had tried to stretch her legs, failed at that, and had kicked a bucket. The clatter it made frightened her and she refused to move after that.

They sat there, sweating, breathing the hot air that

tasted of dust and wondering what was happening outside. The voices came close and then faded. There was noise and then none.

Finally Kehoe whispered, "Can we get out of here?"

Godwin shrugged and said, "You got something to do?"

"No."

"Then let's just stay put a few minutes longer."

"It's hot."

"Shit," he said. He knew that it was hot. He could feel that it was hot. He could see it. He wiped at the sweat on his face and wished that he was in Michigan with ten inches of snow and the air so cold that it grabbed at the body. Instead, it seemed that he was slowly melting away.

"How about now?" she asked. She was whining, not liking it in the stuffy closet.

"A few minutes more."

"Why? There's no one out there now. They've already checked this floor."

"Patience," said Godwin. That was something he'd learned at home in Michigan. Patience. The ability to sit quietly and wait for his turn to ride in the go-cart or his turn to select the TV program. He didn't need instant gratification.

Kehoe put a hand on the bucket next to her and levered her way into a standing position. She stood there a moment, pulled the hanging, wet hair off her forehead and looped it behind her ear.

"I'm getting out," she announced.

"Wait!" He started to stand up.

Kehoe slipped, caught herself and grabbed the door-knob. She tossed it open and leaped out.

Godwin followed her and gasped at the relative coolness of the air in the hallway. He took a deep breath and turned.

He was facing a stocky Cuban soldier holding an AK and grinning broadly.

"Whoops," said Godwin.

"Sorry," said Kehoe.

"Vamanos," said the soldier.

Tynan left Carter in her office and walked over to a separate building half a mile away. Walking along the road, he had a chance to see more of the base. White wooden buildings erected in the haste to get the war effort in full gear in the months after Pearl Harbor in 1941. And there were brick and smoked glass buildings. New structures to house the colonels and generals, the captains and the admirals. There were some huge old trees shading parking lots holding the newest and hottest of cars.

Tynan finally reached a small brick building that had two windows in the front, near the door, and no others. There were radio antennas on the roof and there wasn't a sign or a number on it, though the military was usually very good at labeling everything.

He stepped to the door and pulled on it, but it was locked. He saw a button and pressed it. A moment later a tinny voice demanded, "Can I help you?"

"Lieutenant Tynan."

"Wait one."

Tynan turned and looked out over the parking lot. Not one military vehicle in it. Not one older car either. That was the thing about GIs regardless of service. They made it through boot camp, got sent to some good assignment and since the Navy provided food, shelter, clothes, and good pay, the first thing the kid did was buy a new car. A hot new car.

There was a buzz at the door and the voice said, "Come on in, sir."

Tynan grabbed the knob, turned it and pushed. He stepped into a small hallway, tiled in green, painted in pale green and brightly lighted. There was a glass case to the right holding a display of old military equipment and photographs.

"Would you come with me, sir?"

Tynan saw a man in Army fatigues and no other insignia. A tall, thin man with light hair, a narrow face and a large nose. "Come with me please," he said again.

Tynan followed him down the hall to a large, brightly lighted room. "In here please."

Tynan entered. There was a lunch table and four chairs around it. A couch was pushed up against one wall and there were metal folding chairs against another. On a metal stand was a small television. A white refrigerator was shoved into a corner. There were three men in the room, all dressed the same, in Army fatigues. Tynan didn't recognize any of them.

"Captain Owens told me my team would be assembled here," said Tynan.

"Yes sir," said the man who'd escorted him in. "That would be us."

"Oh no," said Tynan. "No offense, but I put in a specific request for specific people."

The escort handed Tynan an envelope and said, "Captain Owens sent this along. My name's Hatcher, Thomas W. Sergeant First Class."

"Sergeant?" said Tynan. "You look young to be a sergeant first class."

"Twenty-eight."

"Okay. Have a seat and I'll see what Owens has to say." He ripped open the envelope, pulled out a chair and sat down. There was a single sheet of paper holding a single typewritten paragraph. He read it quickly.

"Son of a bitch."

"Sir?"

"I take it, Hatcher, that you're the senior man here?"

"Yes sir."

"What's your training?"

Hatcher scratched his head. "Varied. Airborne school, of course. Ranger training and a hitch at the Unconventional Warfare School at Bragg for communications. Cross trained in intell."

"Familiar with the Cuban military?"

"Yes sir."

Tynan nodded and waved at the other men in the room. "Who do you have with you?"

Hatcher pointed. "Man on the end. The robust guy is Sergeant Ralph Blanchard. Skinny kid next to him is Bill Featherman, and last is Bruce Smith."

"Ranks?"

"Both are corporals."

"Gentlemen," said Tynan looking at them, "I requested a team of trained Special Forces men, more specifically, SEALS whom I have worked with in the past."

"We're all airborne qualified," said Hatcher.

"Sergeant, you know that jumping out of an airplane is not the same as getting Special Forces training. Airborne school is three weeks . . ."

"Sir," interrupted Featherman, "we've been through more than just the airborne school. Now I haven't been to the Unconventional Warfare School, but I have had some ranger training and survival training."

Tynan shook his head. "And it's fine training too, but I had something else in mind."

"I can handle anything that you can sir."

Tynan stared at the man, but he wouldn't look away. His pride had been injured. Tynan had only meant that the ranger school was a good base to build on, but without further training or combat experience, it was only a base.

"You been to Vietnam?" asked Tynan.

Featherman shook his head. "No sir."

"Any of you?"

Both Hatcher and Blanchard nodded. Featherman and Smith sat quietly, trying not to be noticed.

Tynan looked at the sheet of paper again. Owens had written that there wasn't the time to scour the country for the men he wanted. There were soldiers located right there who were as well trained as the SEALS. He'd have to use them.

While it might be true that there were soldiers as well trained, he wasn't sure that he had found any. Hatcher, maybe, but the others, no. If he was smart, he'd refuse to be forced into a position of using men he had no confidence in.

"Sir," said Featherman, "even if we all haven't been to Vietnam, we're still good soldiers. We're going to end up there. Is your mission any tougher than that?"

"You people don't have any idea about the mission?"

Now Hatcher took over again. "We were told that a specialized mission, involving men trained for covert operations was in the works. That training was to include jump school and some additional training, such as ranger school. Nothing was said about combat veterans."

"We can do it, sir," said Featherman.

"I'll give you all points for enthusiasm, but that might not be enough."

Now it was Smith's turn. "We can handle the mission sir. It's not like you'll be invading the Soviet Union."

Tynan leaned against the table and pulled the sheet of paper around to look at it. The instructions from Owens were clear. Typical of a man who didn't understand that highly trained men needed to work with other men of equal training. To throw men who were not trained into the mission jeopardized the whole thing. He couldn't count on their reactions. He couldn't count on them.

But the instructions were there, in black and white. He had four men and they were the only ones he was going to be given. He closed his eyes and tried to think his way through it. If the mission was only to go in, find the American students and lead them to the beach for pick-up, then the men should be fine.

There was no reason for him to even think about it. It wasn't corporate America where he could refuse an assignment because it wasn't a good one. He couldn't delegate it so that he would be blameless. The only choice was to take it, make sure that he had everything wired in advance, and go with it.

Tynan nodded and said, "Gentlemen, I want you assembled here at sixteen hundred for a formal briefing. I'll want to see your weapons and your 201 files with a complete list of your training and your qualifications."

"Two oh one files might be difficult to supply, sir," said Hatcher. "The S-1 might not to surrender them."

"Get what you can," said Tynan. "If he balks at that, write it out for me."

"Yes sir."

Tynan stood up and moved toward the door. "I want you here at sixteen hundred. I'll be back then. Questions?" When no one said anything, Tynan nodded. "See you all later."

# 8

The counter-attack by the locals came in the middle of the afternoon. Salinas had spoken to the students, suggesting that they stay in their rooms, and that two people per floor would be allowed to travel to the kitchen for food later. They would have to share what they found there until the situation stabilized. There should be no trouble as long as the students didn't make waves. Transportation home would be arranged as soon as it could be arranged. Salinas promised them that nothing would happen to them. Nothing more, anyway.

And then came the attack.

He had been outside the auditorium, smoking a cigarette and talking to a couple of enlisted men. They heard a noise, like voices in the distance and then there was a single scream. Long, loud and horrifying.

Salinas flipped away his cigarette and demanded, "What was that?"

One of the sergeants shrugged. Salinas slapped him on the arm and yelled, "Come on!"

The soldier jacked a round into the chamber of his AK-47 and followed the officer. They ran around the corner of the building, through a thick hedgerow planted with ferns and broadleaf bushes and came out on the street. A crowd of locals, armed with axes, hoes, bats, crowbars and a few ancient rifles were boiling up the street, screaming, shouting, and attacking anyone who got in their way.

Two soldiers, their weapons held at port arms ran from the shelter of the university buildings. One of them yelled for the crowd to halt, but they didn't listen. As he raised his weapon to fire, they swept over him. An ax flashed and the man screamed. Salinas saw him fall to the street as the crowd swirled around him, kicking, hitting, cutting and slashing. Blood splattered and it ran thick on the pavement.

The second soldier, ten or twelve feet away, fired a single burst. The sound ripped through the air. Two attackers fell, one of them kicking spasmodically. The second dropped like his bones had instantly turned to jelly, dead before he hit the street.

But the mob had taken the weapon of the dead soldier. There was return fire and the second soldier was hit. He dropped his rifle and staggered to the rear. Another burst tore into the stone of the building above his head. He turned then, running to the rear, forgetting about his weapon and his friend.

"Come on," yelled Salinas. He found another three men and they raced down the street. One man threw himself to the ground, firing one single shot. A man with an ax fell, tried to stand and collapsed, spitting blood. Another was hit, rolled to his back and was still.

Now the crowd began to run as those with weapons fired at the Cubans. Salinas pulled his pistol and fired into the middle of the mob. A woman was hit and died with a high pitched wail. Another man fell, rolled and then got to his hands and knees, shaking his head.

Around him, his men were gathering. Now there were a dozen of them, kneeling and firing. The rounds ripping

into the crowd, scattering it. The men with weapons were
shooting, rapidly, trying to cover the retreat.

"Let's go," yelled Salinas, on his feet again. He waved
the men forward.

They ran toward the firing locals. One of the Cubans
took a bullet in the chest. He fell, the blood pumping from
him rapidly, staining the street and creating a pool in the
gutter. Another man was winged. He spun, lost his balance
and fell. Salinas ignored him as they attacked.

The noise of battle increased. They ran toward the
armed men, firing at them. They dodged right and left,
covering each other. Another soldier was hit, pitching forward and tossing his weapon into the street in front of him.

Suddenly the crowd attacked, swinging their weapons.
They rushed forward, a thick mob, screaming their hatred.
In a second, they swarmed around the Cuban soldiers.
There was some firing, but the advantage of the automatic
weapons was suddenly gone. The soldiers couldn't use
them for fear of hitting their fellow soldiers.

"Disengage!" ordered Salinas. "Fall back!"

A man swung a bat at his head. Salinas ducked under in
and pushed the barrel of his pistol into the man's crotch.
He pulled the trigger and felt the weapon fire. Blood splattered him, covering his hand. It splashed up, on his face.
He could smell hot copper as the man shrieked, grabbing at
himself as he dropped to the concrete.

Salinas whirled, slugged a man on the side of the head
and then punched at a heavy woman. She grunted in surprise and hit back, catching Salinas with a glancing blow.
He staggered, and suddenly found himself on the edge of
the crowd. He fired at a young, bearded man blocking his
way. The man fell forward and then curled up into a ball,
moaning in pain.

Salinas leaped over the body. He was suddenly free of

the mob. He fired back into it, shooting the people standing closest to him. When his pistol was empty, he sprinted
down the street, listening to the shouting behind him.
There were occasional shots. A burst and more yelling. As
he reached the corner of the building, he turned. Reloading
quickly, he watched as the fight was flowing up the street,
like the tide moving up the beach, coming closer.

Now he fired until his weapon was empty. As he ducked
back to reload, two men joined him.

"Pick your targets. We have men in there."

They began to shoot single shot. Around them, from
doorways, from the rooftop, and from behind the armored
personnel carriers, more of his men gathered and fired. The
people began to fall. One, two and then a dozen. The return fire was sporadic and poorly aimed.

"That's got them!" yelled Salinas. "Pour it on! Pour it
into the mob."

The crowd began to retreat, slowly at first. They left the
dead and wounded where they fell. Those who could,
grabbed the dropped weapons, picked up the old rifles and
snatched the AKs from the hands of the dead and wounded
Cuban soldiers. As the firing increased, the retreat turned
into a rout. People were screaming in terror. They pan-
icked, trampling those who fell in front of them, not caring
about their wounded friends. Now they only wanted to get
out.

In their wake, they left the bodies of the Cuban soldiers,
a couple of them hacked to pieces. One of the Cubans was
pulling himself toward his friends, one hand and then the
other, looking as if his legs were paralyzed. There was a
lack of terror on his face.

The soldiers ran forward to help their wounded friends.
One of the men was carrying a canvas bag with a red cross

on it. He knelt next to the wounded man and began to treat his wounds with clean bandages.

Salinas moved from the corner of the building, watching as his soldiers moved among the wounded, picked up the weapons that had been left behind. There weren't many of them. One old rifle with the breech looking as if it had been blown apart and a couple of axes.

There were many wounded, most of them locals. The Cuban soldiers had been stomped, stabbed and ripped apart. Salinas reached the first of the wounded locals. A young man with a broken leg. Bone pushed through the skin and the cloth, the tip of it bloodied. He grinned up at Salinas, as if to say that they hadn't meant it, and that he appreciated the medical care he would soon receive.

Salinas looked at the bodies of his soldiers. They were all young men. Studying their ripped and broken bodies, he felt a rage begin to burn in his belly. A white hot pain that spread until he could no longer stand the sight of the locals. People didn't rip each other to shreds. People didn't kill the wounded who were lying helpless.

But once they did, they proved themselves inhuman. They showed that they were not worthy of human considerations. These people, who had killed his soldiers, now expected him to treat their wounds and send them home.

That just wasn't in his make-up.

He aimed his pistol at the face of the man closest to him. The one with the broken leg and who continued to grin, as if showing his teeth would somehow stop the bullet. Salinas squeezed the trigger and felt the weapon fire.

He saw the whole process as if it had been filmed in slow motion. A third eye appeared in the man's forehead. A round, black hole that slowly filled with blood. The back of the man's skull exploded, spraying more blood and brain to the street as his head snapped back sharply. There was a sigh, like air escaping from a tire as the man's body went suddenly rigid and he flopped back.

A moment later there was another shot as another of Salinas's soldiers killed another of the wounded. And then the soldiers moved over the field, shooting the wounded and pumping rounds into the bodies of the dead. Salinas made no move to stop them.

The orgy of killing lasted for ten minutes. Finally the men, exhausted, sickened, and out of ammo, retreated from the field. They collapsed in the warm sunlight, on the soft grass, and stared at the bodies scattered in the street. Some helped carry their wounded friends and the bodies of their fellow soldiers out of the street.

Lieutenant Batista came at him and asked, "What happened here?"

"Riot," said Salinas, not wanting to talk about it. "We turned them around."

"I think it is time to abandon this university," said Batista.

"I think you are right. Round up the students. We can not leave them here. The locals are too angry and would probably attack them. All foreigners look the same."

"And do what with them?"

Salinas stuffed his pistol back into his holster. He wiped the sweat from his face on the sleeve of his uniform. "We will march them to the airfield where we can watch them easily."

"Yes sir." Batista whirled and hurried off.

Salinas watched him go and then looked back down the street where the dead lay. A hundred of them dead? Maybe more. That would teach them the power of the Cuban military. They had learned an expensive lesson, but somehow he didn't think it would take.

Godwin had watched the riot from the window of his room, silently cheering on the locals. He was surprised when the Cuban soldier had fired at them, and had been stunned when the crowd killed him in retaliation. But the most surprising thing was the ruthlessness of the Cubans. They had attacked the civilians with their automatic weapons. They had fired into an almost unarmed crowd and then had walked among the injured shooting them.

It had been a horrible thing to watch, and it had been a fascinating thing. It was almost as if he was seeing it on TV. The people were far away, strangers, and not even Americans. Their deaths didn't bother him as they tried to overrun the Cubans. But then the soldiers had finished off the wounded, and Godwin had thought he was going to be sick.

Kehoe was sitting on the floor, refusing to watch. The shouting, the shooting, the screams of pain and fear did nothing to arouse her curiosity. Once in a while she'd ask, "What's going on out there?"

And Godwin would say, "Riot." She didn't ask for more information.

But then the Cubans had started shooting the wounded and he had turned away. "Christ," he said. "Jesus Christ."

Kehoe still hadn't looked. Godwin returned to his perch and watched as the soldiers finished killing the locals.

"Those bastards," he said. "Those filthy bastards."

"Don't say that," she said. "If they hear you, they'll get mad."

Godwin stood up and moved to the sink. He ran some water into the palm of his hand and threw it on his face. He shook his hand over the sink and then turned to face her. She noticed that he was pale, looking sick.

"You okay?"

"Not after that. I was okay until they started shooting the injured. Just murdering them."

"So what are we going to do?"

Godwin shook his head. "There's not much we can do."

At that moment there was a sound on the stairs and then one of the Cubans ran down the hallway shouting for everyone to move out, to get out, into the hall.

"Now what?" asked Kehoe.

Godwin didn't answer. He opened the door and saw the others were there, watching and waiting. In English that was heavily accented, the soldier announced, "You are no safe here. You must come with me. We go to safety, rapid. You have questions?"

"Are we going to come back here?"

"I do not know."

"Should we take anything with us?"

The soldier shook his head and said, "You come now. Down the stairs."

"We need some information," said Godwin.

The soldier, suddenly frustrated by all the questions, yelled, "You go do now. You move now. No more talk."

A student standing close said, "We've got to have . . ."

The soldier cut him off with a vertical butt stroke. There was a thunk as the wood of the AK stock struck bone. The man clapped a hand to his head as he fell to the floor.

"You go now."

Kehoe looked up at Godwin. He shrugged. "Nothing we can do now except get ourselves into trouble. Let's go."

They joined the line of students filtering down the hall to the stairs. As they entered the stairwell, Godwin whispered, "Stay close to me. We get the chance, we'll get out."

Kehoe nodded, but Godwin wasn't sure they'd get the chance now. It seemed that the Cubans were watching them too closely.

# 9

As requested, the men were assembled in the secure, blockhouse like building. They were still wearing the fatigues that had no insignia. They had struck their gear in the corners, out of the way and sat on the couch or the metal folding chairs. Tynan nodded at them as he entered, took a position near the table and waited as Carter set up her gear.

"This is Captain Jillian Carter of the United States Air Force and she'll be briefing us on the situation on Grande Terre."

She stepped forward. During the day sometime, she'd gone home, changed into an Air Force uniform and returned. Now she stood in front of them, in a short skirt, blue uniform blouse complete with her ribbons and name-tag, and in black high heeled shoes.

"Gentlemen," she said, "the information I have here is classified as secret and shouldn't be discussed outside a secure area or with people not cleared to hear it."

Each of the men nodded. With that, she put up her map and began the briefing, telling the new men what they had learned in the last few hours. They had located, at a travel agency, a brochure that had pictures of the island, a map of the city of San Antonio that showed the relative positions of the university, the airfield, the Presidential Palace, the port, one of the big parks, and a few other landmarks that didn't interest them. While Tynan was running around doing other things, Carter had the brochure's map blown up into a large chart.

She explained the mission as detailed by Owens—what exactly they were expected to do, and when they were expected to do it.

When she finished, Tynan took over. He moved to the front, stood looking at the map as if it was the first time he had seen it. "Can we get this thing reduced?"

"Certainly. I'll have copies made for each of you," she said.

"Thank you," he said. He turned to face his men again and shook his head. Men he didn't know. Men who hadn't been tested under fire. He remembered a graduation exercise for his SEALS that had taken place in Vietnam. Death was a failing grade there. Now he had to deal with men who hadn't seen much more than the average civilian.

"All right," he said. He glanced at his watch and said, "We'll be leaving here, this base, in about four hours. We'll take a C-141 to the naval base at Guantanamo in Cuba." He grinned at that. "Ironic that we'll be staging out of Cuba just as our possible enemy did."

None of the men said anything to that. Tynan shrugged and continued, telling them the schedule of events. They'd be ferried to a submarine and then put out in a rubber boat to the shore of Grande Terre. It was a short walk to the university. They'd run through the dorms, letting everyone know that American sailors and soldiers were there to escort them home and then return to the port facility so that they could get off the island. A naval task force was already steaming toward the island and would be in place within twelve hours.

He finished giving them the briefing, telling them that the opportunity to contact the Cubans was remote. It was strictly a sneak in and get out operation and they were not supposed to see the Cubans.

"Now," said Tynan, "any questions?"

"We know that the Cubans are there, on the island, for sure?" said Hatcher.

"Our man in San Antonio has seen enough of the soldiers and their equipment to identify them. So yes, there are Cuban soldiers there."

"Have they moved on the university?"

"No indications of that, however, we can't assume that the situation won't change before we arrive."

"What happens if we run into a Cuban soldier?" asked Featherman.

"We run away," said Tynan. He locked eyes with the younger man. "The problem here is that we want to avoid contact. If you can, you get out. If you can't, if the situation dictates it, you take him out."

"Meaning?" asked Featherman.

Tynan took a deep breath. "If there is no alternative, you kill him, but I want to stress that we are not there to contact the Cubans. We're going in to get American citizens at the university. That's all we're going to do."

"Anyone else going in?" asked Hatcher.

"We're the first and the only team. We give the Americans at the university an opportunity to get off the island and then we get out."

"They the only group there?" asked Hatcher.

Carter stepped forward and said, "Other concentrations of American citizens have already been evacuated."

"Why?" asked Hatcher.

"That's a good question," said Tynan. He looked at Carter and asked, "Why were the other Americans evacuated?"

"I think I might have given you the wrong impression. The only other concentration of Americans there was a consulate in San Antonio and with the growing tensions, they were ordered out. The students figured that internal politics didn't affect them. They had a chance and they ignored it."

"Damn college students," said Hatcher. "Always causing us trouble."

"They're still American citizens," said Carter. "You have to remember that."

"I wish they would," snapped Hatcher.


Owens sat in his office, surrounded by the top secret documents that detailed the Cuban invasion of Grande Terre. These were CIA reports from an agent on the island and were coupled to reports from Cubans living in their homeland and who were spying against Castro. The whole plan was outlined, including the exact units being used, names of the commanders and their specific duties. Lying on his desk, right under his nose was the detailed plan for Operation Rimfire.

Sitting in the office with him were Commander Marcel and Captain Banse. There were two other staff officers, Lieutenant jg Jack Olsin and Ensign Wilbur Sutton.

Owens sat there, feeling like Eisenhower just prior to the invasion of Normandy. Everything about the operation spread out at his fingertips and he wasn't required to leave his office. His job, and the job of his men, was to monitor the radio traffic coming from the various military units, Army, Navy, Marine and Air Force that were going to participate in the counter-attack of Grande Terre. That was his only mission. Make sure that the communications did not break down.

"Time table is set and the wheels are in motion," he said, glancing at the document. "The task force has been dispatched and is steaming toward its destination. Air Force transports are on stand-by at Eglin and the soldiers are being moved to that location. Scheduled kick off for the whole mess is zero six hundred hours day after tomorrow. Questions?"

"What about the students at the university?" asked Banse. He sat there doing a slow burn. He'd thought that he'd be in command of one of the capital ships heading into harm's way and not sitting around listening to it on the radio.

"They'll be gotten out by that SEAL who was here last night."

"He know that he's been given the babysitting assignment?" asked Banse.

"Nope. He's been told that the Americans must be rescued and that's all he knows."

"What about the pathfinders and the shock troops?" asked Marcel.

"Army's providing their own. I understand that one group will drop on the airport to take it so that the C-141s and C130s can land with the heavy equipment. Better than air landing it in a hostile environment."

Banse sat there and rubbed his face. He didn't like the plan at all. He'd seen it grow from a concern for American lives on Grande Terre to an all out invasion with everyone getting into it. Army and Navy fighting for the juicy roles. Air Force flying cover and bringing in the troops. Everybody had a job and everyone was happy.

Owens pulled a map from the pile of material and held it

up. A rough outline of the island showing a couple of the major roads and the capital city.

"Navy is going into the port, Army landing at the airfield as soon as it is secure and the Air Force to provide close air support."

"What if the Cubans don't roll over?" asked Banse. "What if they call for the Soviets to help them?"

Owens dropped his map to the top of the desk and said, "I would imagine that the President, the Secretary of Defense and of State, have thought this through. We have the right to protect American lives. The Cubans have no right to the island. I would imagine that the Soviets will stay out of it."

Banse shook his head. Owens might be right about the Soviets staying out of it, but it seemed to be a ridiculous chance to take. The Cubans might not have the right to be there, but then, neither did the Americans. The quagmire of Vietnam hadn't taught anyone anything. Everyone believed that a little macho saber rattling would cause the Cubans to beat feet for their own island.

"In twelve hours," said Owens, ignoring Banse, "this base will become a restricted facility. The gate guards will be armed, their weapons loaded and access will be restricted to military personnel, exclusively."

"What about their dependents?"

Owens smiled. "Dependents will either stay on base or they will stay off base. Only military personnel will be allowed to leave and return until our people have secured the island."

"You can't do that," said Banse.

"Of course I can. This is a military facility. The support functions such as the BX and the banking institutions are allowed on for the convenience of the military. Dependents are allowed here for the morale of the troops. They'll have to live with the disruption for four or five days."

Banse shook his head, trying to figure out what was wrong with the picture. Then, suddenly, he had it. They all seemed to be playing Army. Little kids with big plans who hadn't thought them through and didn't care to. Vietnam was dangerous. People were getting killed there. But here was a chance to be brave, be involved in a war with no chance of getting shot. It made him angry, but there was nothing he could do about it.

Owens was going on and on, outlining the invasion plan again, looking and sounding like Patton as he lead the Third Army through Europe. Kid's games.

"The balloon goes up at midnight," said Owens. "We'll begin our operations then and not shut down until the operation has succeeded. Everything manned twenty-four hours a day. Now, are there any questions?"

There were none.

Tynan finished by inspecting the equipment the men had brought with them. The rifles were M-16s, each with the modification that was supposed to clear it if and when it jammed. They had the new thirty round magazines. Hatcher explained that the jamming problem with them had been eliminated and it wasn't as if they were going into the jungle where they needed to control their rate of fire with the twenty round jobs.

Each of them had a combat knife, though those carried by Featherman and Smith were newly issued knives. Neither man had put a razor edge on them. Each of them also had a pistol. Blanchard and Featherman had .38s and Smith had a .45. Only Hatcher had a Browning like the one Tynan carried.

They had an assortment of squad equipment such as radios, batteries for them, grenades, and spare ammo. Tynan didn't like the big squad radio and suggested that

Hatcher try to find some of the small URC-10s so that everyone could have a radio.

"No problem," he said.

Tynan inspected it all, found it all in good working condition and said, "We'll find something to eat and call for transport to the airfield."

"We going to have a chance to make some phone calls?" asked Featherman.

"Christ, no!" said Tynan. "As of now, we're staying together until we get back."

"But I've got a date tonight and I can't stand her up."

"Tough shit," said Hatcher.

"No," said Featherman. "You don't understand. I can't stand this girl up." He glanced first at Tynan and then Hatcher and finally back to the Lieutenant.

"She'll understand," said Tynan.

"Maybe. But maybe she won't. Wouldn't it be better if I gave her a quick call to cancel the date rather than let her speculate about what might be going on?"

Tynan shrugged and Carter said, "I think he's right. It'd be better if he canceled the date, rather than just stood her up."

"Anyone else?" asked Tynan.

The others shook their heads.

"Five minutes," said Tynan. "That's all. You tell her that you can't make it because the duty roster has been changed due to illness and you can't get out of it. That's all you tell her. You'll call her as soon as you can. That's it."

"Yes sir."

Featherman stood and moved toward the door. Tynan stopped him again and said, "If you're not back here in five minutes, I'll be looking for you."

"Yes sir."

Featherman disappeared out the door. Tynan dropped into one of the chairs and said, "Christ, I don't believe it."

Hatcher picked up his M-16, worked the bolt and then sighted on the refrigerator. "In and out," he said.

"Exactly."

# 10

It had been a hot, humid, lousy day. They had to sit on the hard concrete floor of the hangar, ask permission to use the bathrooms, and then had a guard standing around inside there to make sure they didn't try to crawl out the tiny windows or maybe flush themselves down the toilet. They'd been fed at noon, but the food was poor, almost inedible, and the water was warm and tasted of salt. Not the greatest meal.

Godwin hated every minute of it and sat there, watching the Cubans as they worked around the airfield. Once there had been the roar of jet engines, but the plane had apparently flown over and hadn't landed. The Cubans had been excited about that, but only for a few minutes.

They had milled around the floor and watched the students. They had opened one of the hangar's huge doors, but there was no breeze, so it just seemed to get hotter inside. There had been protests, but the students had been told to sit down and shut up. They would be sent home as soon as it could be arranged.

Godwin had stood once, walked toward the hangar door, but had been intercepted before he was halfway across the floor. The guard shouted instructions that he pretended he couldn't understand, but the guard had motioned toward the others with the barrel of his weapon and Godwin had understood that all too well. In his mind he saw the bodies of the wounded as the Cubans killed them and he had no desire to join them in death.

He walked back to where the others sat and joined them as the guard walked away.

"I want to get out of here," said Kehoe.

Godwin thought about the riot in the streets outside of the university, about the shootings and the killings and said, "We're probably better off here." It made him sick to say because he wanted nothing to do with the Cubans now. Not after what he'd seen.

"Under the thumb of the Cubans?"

He looked at the guards and leaned close to her. "They're not shooting at us now. They're here for our protection as well as our jailers. Maybe we should just hang loose."

Kehoe shook her head. "That's how we got here in the first place."

"Which isn't as bad as running around on the streets," whispered Godwin. "At least they're not killing us."

"I want out," repeated Kehoe. "And I plan to get out, with your help or without it."

Godwin looked at her and shook his head. "They can't hold us here forever. The State Department would be filing protests. The Cubans will be under pressure to release us."

"So they file protests and we're still sitting here waiting for someone else to do something."

Godwin shrugged. He had to agree with her. He didn't want to sit around while some pencil dick in Washington filed protests and complained to the Cuban ambassador in the United Nations who would ignore the protest.

Kehoe slipped closer and whispered, "I read a book

once where these people in a similar situation escaped. They just waited quietly until two in the morning, when everyone was tired and then they just slipped away. Moved into the shadows and slipped away."

"We'll see," said Godwin, but he suspected that by two in the morning, she'd be asleep along with everyone else.

"Good." She stretched out and closed her eyes. "We should get some sleep now," she suggested.

"Of course," said Godwin, wondering why she was suddenly so hot to run and why he was so reluctant to. "Of course."

The droning of the jet engines and the darkness in the rear of the aircraft made Tynan sleepy. He looked at the men with him, saw that the old timers, Hatcher and Blanchard, were already asleep. The youngsters were too wired to sleep. They were sitting together, talking at each other, apparently not listening to one another.

But the surprise on the flight was Carter. Tynan had expected to leave her back at the base reading the latest intell and filling in the flight crews that were processing through on their way to Florida, Cuba and then Grande Terre. But Owens had appeared, told Tynan that she would be going with them and then bounced on out.

She'd seemed happy about the situation. Now he expected to ditch her in Cuba. With all the traffic scheduled in and out, he figured she'd just catch a ride on back. Through his squinted eyes, he watched her as she read through the documents she had brought with them. A briefcase full of the latest on the situation on Grande Terre, the unclassified materials they had found, and the maps. She was preparing herself for the upcoming mission.

Tynan got out of his seat and moved over to where she sat. There weren't many seats on the plane. Most of the

space was taken up with equipment and supplies for the
Marines at Guantanamo. The equipment and supplies were
strapped to pallets fastened to the floor and jammed into
the rear of the aircraft. But it left him room to maneuver
and he had the deck space to kneel in front of her.

"Got anything interesting?"

Carter glanced at him and shook her head. "The situation seems to have remained stable since the last updates.
Reports of some rioting but nothing else."

Tynan nodded and held out his hand. She gave him a
number of the documents. Flimsy things on a paper that
felt slippery and smelled of mimeograph ink. He read
through them quickly.

"With luck," he said, "we're in and out. Find the students and lead them to the beach."

"Have you thought about that yet?" she asked.

Tynan stood and took the seat next to her. He leaned
close and over the roar of the jet engines said, "Some. If
we're lucky, the students will all be congregated in one of
the largest areas, a student union, auditorium or gym. We
won't have to search the campus for them."

"And if they're not?"

"Once we find a couple of them and identify ourselves,
we'll have their help in finding the others. It's not like
they'll be hiding from us."

Carter nodded and then said, "But you have to remember that this is not normal times. They'll have seen the
Cubans landing and they'll have heard the shooting in the
streets. They may be hiding, if not from us, then from the
Cubans."

"Even so," said Tynan, "it's not that difficult a task.
And once we've located one or two, they'll be able to help
us find the rest."

"I suppose," she said.

"One thing," said Tynan. "That paper you have there tell you how many students we're suppose to be searching for?"

"No current lists of students are available." She grinned. "But the consulate building will have a record of all visas granted to the students."

"Terrific," said Tynan.

Carter nodded and said, "But your general idea, of the students helping us holds true. Once they realize we're there to get them off the island, they'll help find their friends. The American student community can't be that large. They'll know everyone."

Tynan leaned back in the chair and closed his eyes. He thought about the mission again. First it was some kind of assassination and then sabotage and now a simple rescue. People running around making decisions without waiting for all the facts. There were questions that occurred to him that no one had thought to ask before. Not one person had said a thing about a list telling them who was in the university. A number had been thrown around, but no one had tried to find a list of names.

"I did find a map of the campus," said Carter. "It's three years old and there has been some construction going on, but we do have a map."

Tynan opened his eyes and looked at her. "Let me see it."

She handed it to him and he studied it. The campus wasn't very large. There were four major structures, built on the four corners of the campus. Two of them were L-shaped. Other, smaller buildings were scattered around the perimeter and with very little effort it would be possible to cut off the passages between the buildings making the campus into a fort.

In the center were other buildings. Low, one, two and

three story structures were built there. There were labels on them, telling Tynan the function.

"This is great."

"I thought you'd like it."

"Get copies made for everyone when we get to Guantanamo."

"Of course." She closed her folder and turned so that she could stare at him. "You know, of course, that I'll be going in with you?"

"What do you mean you'll be going in with us?" asked Tynan.

"I'll be heading to the island with you and to the university."

Tynan thought quickly and said, "I thought you'd be staying at Guantanamo."

"Captain Owens suggested that I head on in with you. As an intelligence officer, I'll be looking for things that you wouldn't notice. Important information for the follow on missions, if there are any."

Tynan took a deep breath. "You're not trained for combat operations."

"You said that it wasn't going to be a combat operation. A sneak and peek job."

Tynan rubbed his face, suddenly feeling sick to his stomach. It wasn't that he believed she was incapable of handling her job, it was that she hadn't been trained for this sort of thing. Sitting in an office and analyzing the intelligence data was different from collecting it. Running through darkened streets where there were hostile locals was different than walking down the hallways and corridors of office buildings.

"You're not talking," she said.

"No," agreed Tynan, "I'm not. I'm a little concerned about this new development."

"Why? You said that Featherman and Smith were inexperienced and they're going in."

"That's different."

"Because they're men?"

"No, because they've had some training. Basic for them taught them to fire weapons, clean weapons and some hand to hand combat skills . . ."

"I've had all that."

Tynan glanced at her. She wasn't a small woman, but then, she wasn't a big one either. She might know enough unarmed combat to hold her own in a fair fight, but they weren't going into a fair fight. Street fighting was different. The point of it was to kill or cripple the enemy quickly and rules didn't apply. He told her that.

"But you said there wouldn't be any fighting."

Tynan nodded and said, "That is my hope, but in these things you can never tell."

"I'm going," she said. "I have my orders."

There was nothing that Tynan could do about it. She was a military officer, she did have orders, and they weren't going into a combat zone. They were sneaking onto a semi-peaceful island to rescue American citizens. Of course, they were going in armed, rounds locked and loaded, but that didn't make it a combat zone.

"You have any training in clandestine operations?"

"Meaning?"

"Do you know how to walk without making noise? Do you know how to slip up to a building without being seen? Do you know how to use the shadows to conceal movement or that sometimes it'll take an hour or more to move a hundred yards?"

She glanced away, at the deck of the aircraft and then turned back, looking him in the eye. "I know enough to follow the lead."

"There anything I can say that would talk you out of this?" asked Tynan.

She shook her head. "I've my orders. Owens gave me written instructions in case you balked, but said not to pull them out unless you demanded them in writing."

"You have a weapon?"

"No. Owens said that I wasn't authorized to carry a weapon," she said.

"Marvelous," said Tynan. "Fat ass sits in his office and decides that you're supposed to land with us, but then tells you not to carry a weapon. Well, I wouldn't do that to my worst enemy. We'll get you a pistol. I assume that you know how to fire one."

"Christ," she snapped, "I'm not an invalid. I can fire a pistol. I've had some training."

"Thank God for small favors."

"I get the impression that you're not thrilled with having to drag a woman along on this."

"No," said Tynan, "not a woman, but an untrained, untested officer. It would be better for everyone if you stayed behind because we're going to have to keep an eye on Featherman and Smith, as it is, and they've had some training."

The loadmaster came around then and said, "We're getting ready to land. I need you to buckle in."

"Of course," said Tynan.

When the man left, Carter looked at Tynan and said, "You're going to let me go along?"

"Hell," said Tynan, "you've got your orders and I've got mine. I think it's foolish and it's typical of the thinking of the managers infiltrating the military now, but if you feel you have to go, I'm not going to stop you."

"Thanks, Mark," she said.

He shot her a glance. "I didn't know you even knew my first name."

"I looked it up," she said.

And then the noise inside the aircraft increased as they began the approach to Guantanamo. And there didn't seem to be anything more to say.

# 11

When the plane landed, they were met by a deuce and a half and two enlisted men with orders to load everything into the rear of the truck. Tynan and his men pointed out their gear, moved it to the hatch and then handed it down to the other men who tossed it up into the truck. That finished, everyone climbed out of the airplane and without a moment to stretch or sightsee, climbed into the rear of the truck.

The air was hot and humid and smelled of salt. The little activity, climbing from the rear of the aircraft and into the rear of the truck was enough to work up a sweat. It stained their uniforms quickly under the arms and down the back.

Then, in the rear of the truck, with the canvas cover pulled down so that no one off the airfield would see them, they drove away. The stench of diesel fuel blew up under the cover, making it hard to breathe. The sun baked the canvas, radiating through it and making life inside even more miserable. No one felt like shouting over the roar of the diesel engine.

They lurched to a stop and the rear flap was thrown up, out of the way. An officer in whites stood there, looking in. "Lieutenant Tynan?"

"Yes."

"Come with me, please."

"What about the men?"

"They can wait right here, or inside if they'll be more comfortable."

Tynan looked into the sweating faces and said, "I want someone to keep an eye on our gear at all times. You can do it from inside, but someone has to watch it."

Hatcher nodded and said, "Aye aye, sir." He grinned broadly as he said it.

"You come with me, Captain Carter."

"Yes sir."

Tynan moved to the rear and dropped from the rear of the truck. He was about to reach up to help Carter and then realized that she'd have to make it on her own once they got to the island. If she was going to hit the island with them, she'd better learn quickly that things were going to change for her.

When she was on the ground, the officer introduced himself. "I'm Lieutenant Commander Higgins. I was told to meet you here and provide any assistance that you might need."

Carter was the first to speak. "I'd like to see the latest intell on the situation."

"In my office," said Higgins. "The latest traffic from the area."

"And a Coke," said Tynan. "I'd like to have an ice cold Coke."

"In my office."

He turned and led them to a metal door in the side of a brick building. As he opened it, Tynan turned and saw that all the others were now on the ground, outside the truck. He was going to order them, again, to watch the equipment, but figured if they couldn't do that right, he was in trouble. Instead he followed Higgins and Carter into the building. There was a concrete and metal staircase that led up to the second floor. The concrete had been heavily waxed and now had a bright brown luster to it.

Then came a fire door and Higgins opened it. They turned to the right where there was a heavy door. On it was a warning that the facility was restricted and unauthorized entry was prohibited by order of the facility commander.

Through it and to the right was another door. Higgins used a key to open it and then turned on the lights. He gestured at one of the chairs and said, "Have a seat."

Carter moved to it and sat down.

The office was long and narrow with two desks pushed against the walls. There was a bookcase against the wall, maps of the world and Cuba hanging up, a clock that was broken and several chairs. The floor was green tile, dirty, and the walls were a pale yellow. Another door led into another room where, Tynan believed, were the files and the safes.

Higgins picked up the phone, dialed four numbers and said, "I want three Cokes in here." He hung up. "Cokes are on the way."

"Thank you."

Higgins sat behind one of the desks, folded his hands and said, "What all have you been told?"

Tynan grinned and didn't say a word. When Carter started to speak, he snapped, "You never compromise the mission."

"Ah," she said.

"All right," said Higgins. "Do you have any specific questions?"

"What's the latest from the island?"

He stood and said, "Let me get the traffic." He disappeared into the rear room and returned with a thick folder.

As he handed it to Carter, there was a knock on the door. He opened it, got the Cokes and passed them out.

Tynan took his, popped the top and drank deeply. "I needed that."

Carter took hers, set it aside and continued to read the messages. She finished and asked, "Is that all?"

"What were you expecting?"

"Protests from half the countries in the United Nations, for one thing. Hostile remarks from our government and some kind of feeble explanation by the Cubans."

"The world diplomatic community has been very quiet about this. Right now, it looks like an internal coup fired by the Cubans."

"And no one is protesting?"

"I think," said Higgins, lifting his Coke and opening it, "that the world is waiting to see which way the wind is blowing."

Tynan leaned forward. "Anything on the students at the university?"

Higgins shook his head. "Nothing new. There was a riot in the streets outside, but there didn't seem to be any involvement by the students. A number of the locals were killed by Cuban soldiers."

Tynan finally looked over at Carter. "You get everything you need?"

"Everything that was to be gotten." She looked back at Higgins. "Anything else?"

"One fly over by recon. Aerial photos don't show much. No aircraft on the runways or taxiways at the airport. No signs of Cuban soldiers except for two APCs outside the Presidential Palace. Everything looks very low key and laid back. They respond with force but they're not out looking for trouble."

"You got a good aerial photo of the city?"

"Yeah."

"Let me have one," said Tynan.

"I can't let you have it, but I can let you see it," said Higgins.

"Any objections to us using it to produce a map?"

Higgins shook his head and said, "You can't copy classified material."

"Commander," said Carter, "you won't let us have a photo and I understand it. That photo gets out and it suggests to the trained observer just how good our aerial recon capabilities are. But if I draw a map, they can't know where I got the data for the map. For all anyone knows, I wandered the streets of San Antonio making my map."

He looked at her and said, "Would you let me do it if our positions were reversed?"

"I understand your reluctance, but this can't hurt."

Higgins nodded and then got up. He returned with a stack of photos in a manilla folder. "Anyone ever asks, you didn't get them here."

Carter took the package and moved to the other desk. She laid the pictures out and then compared them to the maps that she had brought with her. Tynan joined her and looked over her shoulder as she tried to make sense out of it.

She pointed at one of the pictures and said, "There's the university, the Presidential Palace, the parks, port and the airfield."

"Okay. Any surprises?"

She shook her head. "No." She pulled on the drawer, opened it and took out a sheet of paper she found there. Quickly, she sketched the downtown area, marking the streets.

Tynan watched her and then said, "I wish we had some street names. Make it very simple to get in there."

Carter pointed to her simple map and said, "The campus is big enough that we could come ashore north of the port and follow the streets until we hit it. No real problem."

She kept working and when she finished, "Can I get some copies made?"

Higgins moved over, looked down at the map and then said, "Take a few minutes."

"Fine," said Tynan.

Higgins made a phone call and someone came to the door. He gave the clerk the maps and told him to make five copies of it. She also gave him copies of the university map she had. The man left quickly. And returned within five minutes, giving back the maps.

As Higgins passed them on to Tynan, he asked, "Is there anything else you need?"

Carter shrugged and Tynan said, "You've given us the latest intell updates?"

"Everything I have, you've seen."

"I guess that takes care of it then."

"Then let's get your men and equipment together and I'll escort you over to the docks."

Tynan moved to the door, as did Carter. He opened it, let her out and then was followed by Higgins who locked his door. They went down stairs and on outside to where the truck waited, but the men were gone. Tynan stood there, looking up into the rear of the truck.

A moment later, Hatcher approached him. "We ready to go, sir?"

"Get the men and hop aboard."

Hatcher waved his arm and the others appeared an instant later. "We've been watching."

They climbed into the truck. Tynan watched and then turned to Higgins. "Thanks for your assistance."

"Good luck."

Tynan hoisted himself up, into the truck. He sat down as Hatcher reached out and dragged down the canvas flap, wrapping them all in semi-darkness.

Carter took out the maps she had made and handed one to each of the soldiers. They looked at them and Carter pointed to the one she held.

"You can see the university and the route from the water to it. The building marked with the plus is the auditorium and the one with the star is the gym. With luck, we'll find the majority of the students there."

"And without luck?" asked Blanchard.

"We get the rare and unique opportunity to search for them," said Tynan.

They fell silent as the ride got bumpy and then smoothed out. They came to a stop and one of the doors in the cab slammed. The driver appeared, peaking under the flap.

"We're here, sir."

Tynan stood up and moved to the rear. Again he dropped to the ground and turned, looking. He'd expected to see a destroyer on the dock. Maybe a cruiser, but not a submarine. Infiltration on subs had gone out with the OSS and World War II. At least that was what he'd told himself. Even as he had joked about a sub infiltration, he'd believed that they would be deployed by a surface ship.

As he stood there an officer in khakis walked over. "You Lieutenant Tynan?"

"That's right."

The officer gestured at the sub and said, "Your taxi is waiting for you."

"You sure this is right?"

"Got sealed orders for you on board."

Tynan slapped the side of the truck. "All right, everyone out." He glanced at the submariner. "We've got a woman traveling with us."

Now the man grinned. "This is not a pig boat from the Second World War. We can handle it."

"You're calm enough about it," said Tynan.

"Not often we get to travel with women."

The men got out of the truck and passed out the equipment. Tynan grabbed his share. When they were ready, the officer said, "If you'll follow me."

They walked out on the dock, up the gangplank and saluted the officer of the deck and the flag. As they stepped on board, a sailor took the gear and moved it to a forward hatch where they dropped it down, into the interior of the ship.

The captain moved forward, holding out his hand. "Welcome aboard, Lieutenant. I'm Commander Dickens."

"Commander," said Tynan. "How soon before we're underway?"

"Wasting no time," said Dickens. "Just as soon as we can get you below. We'll be in position within twenty-four hours. You'll be going ashore tomorrow evening."

"Not soon enough for me," said Hatcher looking up at the conning tower.

"You don't like subs?"

"No sir." Grinning, he used the old joke. "I like to sleep with the windows open."

The captain didn't bat an eye. He said, simply, "So do I."

# 12

It turned out to be a miserable night. Hot and uncomfortable, with Cuban soldiers watching every move that everyone made. Godwin sat there, wishing that there was something to do. A book to read or a radio to listen to. He wished that he had some of the beer that Vicki had gotten from her brother. He wished that there was something to think about, other than armed men watching them and ordering them around. He wished there was a way to take his mind off the people murdered by the Cubans. But every time he forgot about it and closed his eyes, there was the scene again. Cuban soldiers walking among the wounded, pistols and rifles in hand, shooting the helpless and the injured.

There were almost no lights on in the hangar. When the sun set, that was it. The Cubans moved everyone to the center of the floor, turned on tiny lights on the perimeter so that anyone trying to get out would have to cross a band of dim light, and then left them alone. It was almost as if they were daring the students to try to escape.

They were given some food. More of the C-ration canned food that didn't taste good. It was more like canned paper and mud, but Godwin was hungry, so he ate it. And drank some of the lukewarm water.

Kehoe refused to eat. She refused to talk and refused to look at their captors. As the sun disappeared, she realized that there was no way for her to escape. The Cubans had thought of everything and watched them all carefully. Now that it was night, they rotated the guards every hour, not giving any of the soldiers a chance to go to sleep while assigned to the guard detail.

Godwin sat in the middle of the floor, looking out the door of the hangar. He could see a portion of the sky to the south. There was a sliver of airfield visible and occasionally one of the Cuban vehicles drove by.

About midnight, there was firing somewhere in the disance. Soft pops and the ripping of cloth as the Cubans and the locals fought it out. There was a string of ruby colored tracers that climbed into the night sky, almost like fireworks on a Fourth of July evening. A couple of flares hung in the sky to the south describing smokey arcs under their parachutes as they drifted lower.

Godwin didn't move. He wanted to stand in the door and look out, much like a man watching the approaching of a thunderstorm, but he knew the guards wouldn't let him. They would force him back, out of the way.

The battle seemed to ebb, the shots becoming random as they seemed to come closer. There was a single, loud explosion that sounded like dynamite going off not far away.

Kehoe sat up with the noise and glanced at Godwin. "What was that?"

"I don't know. Someone blew something up."

She shook her head and hissed, "I hope it was someone blowing up a bunch of Cubans."

"I'm not sure that we should feel that way. So far the

Cubans have protected us." Even as he said it he again remembered the Cubans shooting the wounded.

"And the Romans protected the Christians right up until the time they threw them to the lions."

Godwin grinned but didn't laugh. "Our situation isn't quite that dramatic."

Kehoe looked around them. More guards near the doors. A few who roved, looking for signs that the students were planning an escape. No way to get out. She lay down again, folding her hands under her head.

"You give up on the great escape?" asked Godwin quietly.

"Nope," she said. "Tonight's not the night. They're too alert."

Godwin had to agree with that. Tomorrow, if no one caused trouble, the Cubans would relax a little. Maybe they could get out then.

He stood and as he did, one of the guards came over. Godwin pointed at the bathroom and said, "Gotta whiz."

"Que?"

"Take a leak. Hit the head. Go to the bathroom. Over there," he said pointing.

The guard nodded and Godwin walked across the floor. Inside the bathroom, he banged one of the doors on the stalls, but instead walked to the window and looked out. No way to open it to climb out without breaking the glass, but he could see out, to the south. The firefight seemed to have ended. There was a fire burning, the black smoke climbing into a grey sky, the flames reflecting on the smoke.

He left the bathroom and returned to the group. He pulled over a jacket, wadded it up for a pillow and lay down. Kehoe was right. Tomorrow would be better. He closed his eyes, listened to the sounds around them and was asleep in minutes. It had been a long, frightening day.

It was mid-morning when Dickens awakened Tynan, telling him, "We're getting close to the destination."

Tynan sat up carefully so that he didn't bump his head on the low hanging bunk above him. He swung his feet over the edge and looked up at Dickens. "What's going to happen?"

"We'll hold our position about ten miles off the coast and stay submerged. After dark, we'll run in submerged, and then surface to put you into the water."

Tynan stared at the floor and rubbed his face quickly. "Can I use the wardroom for a classified briefing this afternoon. Take thirty minutes at the most."

"That's no problem."

Dickens sat down in the chair near the little built in desk. "Can I ask you a question?"

"Shoot."

"How in the hell did you get mixed up in this mess? Soldiers and a woman?"

"I've asked myself that question too." Tynan looked up and grinned, but wished the sub captain would leave him alone for a few minutes. Long enough for him to shake the sleep out of his head and grab a drink of water. Maybe a glass of orange juice. Something.

"I think I'd opt out of the mission," said Dickens.

"If that was an option, which this isn't. Besides, I don't think we're going to have that kind of problem."

Dickens stood up and said, "When you're ready, I've some sealed orders for you to look at. I was told to hold them until noon today, but if you won't tell that I gave them to you early, I won't either."

"Thanks, Captain. As soon as I can get into a uniform I'll be ready."

Dickens disappeared through the curtain and Tynan forced himself to stand up. He could hear the rumbling of the engines, feel the vibrations through the deck, and knew that they were underway. The air was cool, but had an under odor to it. A canned flavor that tall buildings in which no windows opened sometimes had. He knew that they were submerged at the moment and breathing recycled air.

He pulled on a fatigue uniform that had black camouflage markings on it in a pattern known as tiger stripes. He thought about a sidearm but figured it would look strange on the sub. He had thought about socks, but rejected the idea. Sitting on the bunk again, he put on his boots, lacing them tightly.

He moved from his cabin to the passage and then down toward the miniature galley. The captain sat there, drinking coffee and reading the official mail. He saw Tynan and asked, "You ready?"

"Can I catch a glass of orange juice?"

The captain slipped to the right, stood and found a moisture beaded pitcher. He poured the juice and handed it to Tynan. "Now?"

"You seem anxious to get rid of the envelope."

"And you seem reluctant to take it."

Tynan sipped his juice and grinned. "Have you ever gotten anything in sealed orders that wasn't bad news?"

"Good point."

Tynan finished the juice and handed the empty glass back to the captain who stored it so that it wouldn't get broken. Then, leading the way, the captain moved toward the stern of the boat. Once in the captain's cabin, he opened his safe and pulled out the sealed envelope.

"You know," he said, "I'm supposed to see your ID before I hand these over."

"Keep them," said Tynan, showing Dickens his military ID card anyway.

"No thanks." He passed Tynan the envelope and then stepped around him so that he could get out of the cabin. "When you've read them, please join me in the galley again."

"Aye aye."

As the captain disappeared, Tynan ripped open the envelope and thought about all the other times in the last few hours he'd been handed an envelope with instructions inside. Bad news, every one of them.

He read through the document and felt the anger bubble through him. He wanted to scream and punch the bulkhead. He wanted to rip them up and pretend that he'd never seen them. They were another example of paper pushing managers not thinking things through. Suddenly, just like that, they were back on one of the original missions and there was no way, given all the circumstances that Tynan could carry out his new orders. Just no way.

Tynan stood leaning against the bulkhead of the tiny wardroom and facing the four men and one woman of his team. He looked into each of their faces as they had entered and then sat down. It was surprising that none of them had gotten sea sick yet, but then the water was calm, the boat seeming to be at a standstill.

When they all assembled, Tynan went over and closed the water tight door. He then returned to his position at the head of the table and said, "This will be our final briefing before we hit the island. I'll talk us through the mission once and then have each of you brief it back to me, making sure that everyone understands it."

He looked at them and then began, running through it. A simple plan that put them ashore, into the campus and then out to the shoreline. They would spend no more than an hour at the campus. They would round up everyone they could find, question them about others, and get the hell out.

Hatcher ran through it, using one of the maps created by Carter. He added a little detail, making it clear that he understood. There was also the suggestion that if the team had to be split into two parts, Hatcher would take charge of one of them.

When they finished that, Carter looked at Tynan and asked, "What were in the sealed orders?"

Tynan laughed. "Yeah, it comes back to that." He glanced at each of the men and said, "I don't want to offend anyone here, but you all know that I was less than thrilled with the make up of this team. It wasn't a major problem because, we were just going to sneak in and get out again."

"So what's the problem with that?"

"Nothing," said Tynan, "but someone up the pipeline somewhere looked at our mission and decided to expand the scope of it."

"How?" asked Carter

"This is what I mean by managers instead of leaders. They figure that since we're going in, and they've now identified one of the Cuban leaders, we should take him out."

The blood drained from Carter's face. Her skin turned waxy and it sounded as if she could no longer get a breath. "What's that mean?"

"They want us to kill the Cuban leader."

"No," she said. "No way."

Tynan looked at her and said, "You're right. No way. But not for the reason you think."

"Why not?" asked Smith.

"Oh, don't be ridiculous," snapped Hatcher. "We don't have a team set up. We don't have the weapons for it and I don't know if anyone here has the training for it. You can't just go waltzing in there and open fire."

Smith sat there looking as if he didn't understand.

"An assassination," said Tynan, "is not a wild man with a rifle, but a coordinated team with a high powered weapon. They know where the target is and they might wait for a week before they can make a shot. It is not something you can do while trying to rescue students. It's not something you can tack on to one mission."

"So, what are you going to do?" asked Carter.

"The assassination attempt failed," said Tynan. "We had to get the students out. Sorry."

"You can do that?" asked Smith.

"Unless one of you say anything stupid, we're in the clear. We couldn't make the mission. End of discussion." Tynan looked at his watch. "Anyone have any questions now?"

"What time do we jump off tonight?" asked Hatcher.

"Hit the boat about twenty-three hundred. Take us two hours to get to the island. We should be able to get out and back by six. Now, anything else?"

When no one spoke, he said, "Couple of final items. First, I hope that I don't have to remind you that we carry no identification on this mission. No wallets with ID cards and no ID tags. Make sure that unit insignia are removed from your fatigues, if necessary, and tear out the tags in them. I want nothing with a US stamp on it except the weapons."

Happy with their response to that, Tynan said, "The last thing is the radio codes we'll use. I'm Diamond One and Captain Carter is Diamond One Alpha. Hatcher, you're Diamond Two and Blanchard, you'll be Three, if we split the team that small. Featherman, you're Two Alpha and Smith you're Three Alpha. We've no authentication codes and none should be necessary. Now, any last questions?"

He looked at them, but no one said a word. "That's it then. We assemble at twenty-one hundred to get ready. See you then."

One by one the men filed out of the wardroom. When they were gone, Carter asked, "So what are you going to do until tonight?"

"I think," said Tynan, "I'm going to spend the afternoon sleeping."

"Oh," she said.

"Unless I can think of something else."

"Well sit down and we'll see if we can think of something," she said.

Tynan did.

# 13

The day was no better for them. The Cuban soldiers circulated, but refused to talk to them. Godwin asked questions of them, but they ignored him. Some of the others demanded answers, demanded to see the officer in charge, and demanded to be released, and they were ignored too. Food was served at seven, noon and then at five. Cartons of C-rations, some of them with American markings and the labels in English. The cartons were left for those who wanted to eat.

About the middle of the afternoon, one of the officers came forward to talk to them. He stood with his back to the door, rocking on his feet, waiting for everyone to fall silent and then look up at him.

"I am sorry for the inconvenience," he said, in a voice that had only a trace of an accent. "We have made contact with your official representatives. Arrangements are being made for your release."

"When?"

"Very soon. We are most concerned with your safety. There has been some hostile activity and we do not want any of you injured."

One of the men stood up, hands on hips and said, "I'll

take my chances. I'll just head on back to the university, if you don't mind."

"I am sorry, sir, but that can not be allowed. We are now responsible for your safety. If you were injured, even if you had left our protection on your own, we would be held responsible for that. It is better that everyone remain here."

"For how long?" asked a girl.

"A few days." The man held up his hands as if to stop a protest and said, "I know that it is uncomfortable and inconvenient, but it is for your own good."

There were more questions and more demands that they be released and returned to the university. They'd be safe there. Everyone would know where they were. They could leave to go home if they wanted. The Cuban officer listened to their complaints and their suggestions for a long time without getting angry. He allowed everyone who wanted to speak have a turn at it, but when they began repeating themselves, he suggested that the session should end.

Before he left the hangar floor he told them, "It will only be for a few more days. Thank you for your cooperation." Then he walked away refusing to answer any of the questions that were asked of him.

Godwin then moved closer to Kehoe and said, "Think it's time we busted outta here, Lefty."

She glanced at him, not understanding.

He lowered his voice and said, "It's time that we get out of here. They have no right to hold us."

"Okay," said Kehoe, "I'm for it. When?"

"We'll see what things look like tonight. If they slack off, we can get out. If not, maybe sometime tomorrow."

"And do what?"

"Head for the port first and see what ships are docked there. We find an American ship and we get on board. If not, back to the university and use the phones."

She touched his shoulder. "The sooner, the better."

"Yeah," agreed Godwin.

Tynan and his men, along with Carter, ate a quiet meal in the wardroom uninterrupted by the rest of the crew. While they ate, stuffing the food in their faces like it was the last meal any of them would ever get, they discussed the mission a final time. A quick, informal briefing on what would happen that night. Into the university, find the students and then out. No bullshit missions to assassinate Cuban Army officers, no sabotage of Cuban equipment, and no grandstand raids to the airport.

As the food was devoured, Carter said, "I would think that you'll want to eat light before a mission so that you didn't get sick."

"Nope," said Tynan. "You eat as much as you can so that if something goes wrong and you're left hanging in the breeze, you don't have to worry about food for a couple of days."

"Makes sense, I guess," she said.

Tynan finished another plate and pushed it aside. That made three dinners he'd eaten. Three full dinners. As he leaned back, he looked into the faces of the men and asked, "We square on what happens tonight?"

One by one they nodded. All except Hatcher. "Just what happens if we run into a Cuban soldier?"

"You run away, if you can. If you can't, you eliminate him as a threat, but our first order is to get in and out."

He fell silent and looked at each of the men. "I want to make one thing clear," he told them. "We are a combat unit. We avoid a fight if possible, but if we can't, we fight. You run into an enemy soldier and there is nothing you can do but kill him, then that's the way it is. Do not jeopardize the mission because you're afraid to use your knife or rifle. We'll worry about repercussions once we're back out."

"Aye aye, sir," said Hatcher, feeling foolish using the standard Navy reply.

At that moment, Dickens stuck his head in and said, "We're about three miles out now. Any time you're ready."

"Just finishing up here," said Tynan.

The captain left and Tynan looked at his watch. "Thirty minutes, gentlemen. Into the black now."

They all trooped out of the wardroom, heading to their billets to change into the black uniforms. Carter did the same, using the captain's cabin to change. That done, they gathered their equipment and made their way topside. They found the captain on the conning tower. Tynan exited, standing next to the officer who was scanning the distant shoreline with a huge pair of binoculars.

"Another ten minutes," he said, "and we'll be no more than two miles out. I don't want to maneuver much closer than that. Bottom shallows rapidly, and we're taking a chance of hitting coral reefs."

"That's no problem, Captain," said Tynan.

"When you going to be ready to go over the side?"

Tynan studied the shoreline in front of him. The ocean was a light grey and the island a dark black mass that sparkled with only a few electric lights. There were torches, fires, lanterns, and flashlights everywhere, but no electricity. He hadn't expected that. He'd expected a land that was blacked out, with only an occasional light to worry about.

He could see the city rising from the land. Some of it was as black as coal, but some of it a charcoal, highlighted by the stars and the night sky. As his eyes adjusted to the dark, he could see more of the city. The outline was obvious and after studying it on the map for a long time, he was

familiar enough with it to recognize some of the landmarks.

"My people are ready now," said Tynan.

The captain reached out and touched Tynan on the arm.
"I don't want to be telling you your business, but is it a
good idea to take that woman along?"

Tynan laughed. "Not my idea. Orders were written on
high and she is a party to the mission."

"Just like those chairborne commandoes. Never think a
thing through."

"That's what I said."

"Good luck, Lieutenant," said the captain. "I'll be here
until four. I'll be only ten or fifteen miles off the coast after
that and ready to come back tomorrow evening if necessary."

"I appreciate that, Captain. You might need to have
some of your men standing by with boats if we have a large
number of students to transport."

"No problem."

Tynan went below and met with his men again. They
made their way forward and up to the hatch there. With the
help of the sailors on the boat, they got up and out on the
deck. Other sailors launched the rubber raft they would
paddle onto the shore.

Tynan gathered the people around him. All were wearing the black fatigues and each had painted his or her face
with the camouflage grease. That made it even harder for
people to see them in the dark, but in the light, it made
each of them look like something from a horror film.
Tynan couldn't help grinning at the nightmarish faces in
front of him.

"Once we hit the boat, there won't be much talking.
Hand signals. Use your heads. Keep the noise down and
move quickly. We'll stay together until we hit the univer-

sity and then split up if we need to search. Keep the radios off until we split up and then don't use them unless absolutely necessary."

He stopped talking and looked at each of them again. There were so many things that he wanted to say because he didn't know them. He hadn't met any of them until thirty hours earlier and he only trusted Hatcher because Hatcher had Special Forces training. Blanchard had been in Vietnam and that helped a little.

But there was so much to say. Little things that men learned on combat tours that couldn't be taught in all the various schools the military ran. How to walk without making noise, taping down clothing so that it didn't rustle, filling a canteen to the very top so that it didn't slosh around and then drinking it all for the same reason. One man would share his canteen with the others and at the next break it would be someone else's turn to share.

He shook his head and said, "Everyone think everything through. Don't go off half cocked and remember that we're on a rescue mission, not an assault."

Hatcher said, "Yes sir," grinned and changed it to, "Aye aye."

The lights were dimmed and they climbed the ladder up and out onto the deck. The sweet salt air hit them. There was moisture in it. And it was warmer than it had been below where the climate was controlled.

Two sailors stood on the deck, each holding a line to the rubber raft, keeping it tight, against the side of the sub. Tynan moved over, and used the rope ladder to climb down into the bobbing and weaving raft. Once in it, he turned and waited as Carter struggled to get down. When she was in, the others followed, with Hatcher handing down the equipment before he climbed aboard.

"We're ready," said Carter.

"That's the last time I want to hear anyone speaking out loud," warned Tynan.

The sailors tossed the lines down and Hatcher used one of the rubberized oars to push them away from the hull of the boat. Then Blanchard, Featherman and Smith picked up the others and began rowing them ashore.

Tynan watched the sub fall way, at first obvious against the light colored ocean, but then fading into an indistinct blob. The only sound was from the distant crash of the surf against the shore and the noise of the city.

They rowed steadily, moving toward the island. Tynan used his compass and tried to keep them moving straight in. The currents and the light breeze pushed and pulled at them, but Tynan kept them aiming at a tall building almost directly to the west.

Carter sat in the bow, watching as the shoreline came closer. First the island was a smudge and then it began to take on a shape. She could see the city and see the lights and the buildings.

The noise of the surf became louder. Tynan took an oar from Blanchard, letting the man rest. Blanchard finally took over from Featherman who took over for Smith who took over for Hatcher. They rotated the duty so that no one was worn out by the trip from the sub.

Finally they were caught in the surf and dragged along, almost like a surf board in California. They rode the crest of the wave and then slipped down it, pushed along by the speed of the water until they were shoved up to the tide line, high and dry.

They leaped from the raft and dragged it up the beach to where the first of the plants were. There were a few bushes, some palm and coconut trees and then an expanse of grass. Tucking the raft up under a fern with huge, lacy branches, they pulled out the equipment and slipped into it.

Tynan checked his compass and then Carter took out the map she had drawn. In the half light around them, she could see the dark black lines from the felt tip pen and congratulated herself on the foresight she had used to make everything so dark.

Leaning close to Tynan, she said, "Down this street for two, three blocks and then over one. We can't miss it."

Tynan nodded and pointed to Hatcher. The soldier understood immediately. He unslung his weapon and then flipped off the safety. Moving forward, he took the point, keeping to the shadows of the trees and the bushes as they crossed the narrow band of the park behind the ocean.

They spread out with Blanchard bringing up the rear. Tynan stayed close to Carter since she was the only one with no training in combat operations. But she picked up on it quickly, keeping to the shadows, just like Hatcher was doing. When they came to the street and Hatcher moved along the wall of the building, she did the same, being careful not to make noise on the concrete. At the first intersection, Hatcher sprinted across, with Carter kneeling in the darkness watching him and not moving until he was across and safe. Only then did she follow, running hard and bent low.

The rest of them crossed the street and they moved out again. It was like working their way through a deserted city. Almost no light and almost no sound. Once in a while there would be a car or a truck in the distance. But it seemed that the people were gone. Someone had scared them all out of the city.

They crossed another street. The buildings opposite them were as dark as the day they were built. No sign that people lived in them. No lights, no radio, and no voices.

They stopped at the third street. Tynan crouched on one knee and raised a sleeve to his face and patted it dry. The heat and humidity had soaked his clothes as quickly as the spray on the ocean. His chest ached from moving through the city and trying to control his breathing so that he made no sound. He heard the breath rasping in Carter's throat as she gasped, but it was a quiet sound, almost impossible to hear.

Hatcher held up a hand and pointed to the left. Tynan nodded and the soldier turned down the street. They ran along the side of a building, keeping it against their left shoulders. Again they came to a cross street, and this time Hatcher stopped without crossing.

Tynan glanced and saw where they were. He moved up, leaned close to Carter and whispered, "Good job."

"What?"

He nodded at the buildings on the opposite side of the street and said, "We're here."

# 14

For a moment they held there, staring at the darkened university buildings. Tynan had thought, believed, that the American students, along with the other foreigners, would have their own sources of light. He believed they would be armed with battery powered radios, coleman lanterns, and flashlights so that even if the city was dark, they would have some power and some light.

But looking up, at the buildings on the northern side of the campus, that didn't seem to be true. There were no signs that anyone was there. None whatsoever.

Hatcher slipped back and leaned in close. "Now what?" he asked quietly.

"We spread out and search. My next guess is that the students will have holed up together to conserve the batteries and the lanterns."

"Any ideas where?"

"Like I said before, probably in the auditorium and the gym. We'll start there."

"What about the cafeteria?"

"Of course. Follow the food," said Tynan. "We'll check there too. Hatcher, you go with Featherman, Blanchard you're on Smith and I'll work with Carter."

119

"Naturally, you get the good duty," said Blanchard shaking his head.

"We don't need all this unnecessary talking," said Tynan. "Keep the radios turned on but turned down, and report back here in one hour."

Hatcher nodded, waited for Featherman to join them and then ran across the street, disappearing into the dark around the campus. Blanchard hesitated, giving Hatcher a chance to get out of the open and then followed with Smith.

"Now us?" asked Carter.

Tynan nodded and said, "Leave your weapon on safe. We don't want to shoot unless we have to and don't shoot into a shadow unless you've identified a target."

"I understand." She started to get up.

Tynan grabbed her, stopping her. "Hold it. Now, we've two groups to worry about. The Cubans and the locals. Remember that. The enemy is all around us. We have to move quickly and quietly. No unnecessary talking and no unnecessary motion."

"Understood."

"Then follow me."

Tynan ran across the street, saw a big black shadow and dived into it. He followed it along the edge of the building and came to a corner. When he stopped, Carter almost ran into him. She stepped back then.

Now they headed across the open ground, dodging right and left, using the shadows, the trees and the bushes for cover. They stopped near a low building. Tynan crawled up under a window and listened, but there was no noise from inside. It was as quiet as a tomb.

They slipped along it, through a garden filled with ferns, broadleafed bushes and small flowering plants. The ground was soft, damp and they sunk into it. Tynan ignored it as he pushed through, came to the other side and ran across a sidewalk. Carter stayed close to him.

They reached another low building, this one as dark and quiet as all the others. Tynan peeked into a low window, but there was nothing to see.

As he turned back toward Carter, there was a shot. A single shot that sounded like an M-16 and then a burst of an AK. Tynan tried to spot the muzzle flashes or tracers. He could see nothing.

To Carter he said, "That's one of our guys and one of the Cubans."

"How can you tell?"

"Sound of the weapons. Each rifle makes a distinct sound when it fires."

There were two more shots from the M-16.

Tynan ran to the corner of the building and looked to the west. He saw a shape running in the shadows and then dive for cover. A moment later another man appeared, following the first. Tynan watched but couldn't shoot. He didn't know who they had run into.

There was a shout in Spanish. And then two more men appeared. Tynan felt Carter pressing against him. He reached out and pushed her back, behind the wall.

One of the running men stopped, knelt and fired. A quick burst that illuminated him like the strobbing of a flashbulb. The outline was of a man in a light colored uniform holding an AK. An enemy soldier shooting at his men.

Tynan swung his own weapon around, hit the selector switch and then aimed by looking over the top of the barrel. He pulled the trigger, felt the light kick of the M-16. The enemy soldier took the burst in the side, flipping away and tossing his weapon into the air.

As he died, his partner opened up, shooting at Tynan.

He heard the snap of the bullets as he ducked back. A couple of rounds slammed into the wall near his head.

"What's happening?" demanded Carter. She was crouched with her back against the wall, the piston against her shoulder and the barrel pointed up, toward the sky.

From a darkened patch came a quick burst. An M-16 that flashed, lighting the bushes around him. The second of the enemy soldiers fell then. Neither of them moved.

Tynan whipped out his radio and hit the transmit button. He whispered, "Diamond two, this is Diamond one."

"Go one."

"Say situation."

"Clear of the campus with negative results. Firing to the south and east of us."

"Roger. Diamond Three, say situation."

"Roger one. Contact with Cuban forces. Fired on and fire returned."

That wasn't quite how Tynan remembered it, but that didn't matter now.

"Understand you are to our right," said Diamond Three.

"Roger," answered Tynan. "Any success?"

"Negative results."

Tynan nodded and keyed the mike. "Withdraw to original location."

"Roger."

Tynan collapsed the antenna and stuffed the radio back into his pocket. He glanced at Carter and said, "Let's get out of here."

"What about the students?"

"They're not here."

"Where are they?"

"Hell, I don't know. Let's just fall back and we'll worry about that later."

Tynan peeked around the corner, saw no movement and then took off running across the open ground. There was a patch of blackness and Tynan dived into it, rolling to his belly. He saw Carter cutting across the grounds and then saw a man seem to rise up from the planting to their right. He knew that none of his men would be doing that. They were either already off the campus or trying to get off. They were not standing around watching the exfiltration.

There was no time to try to identify the target. No time to think about it. No time to plan for it. He aimed and pulled the trigger. Five quick shots.

The shape disappeared without firing in return. The way it vanished, Tynan knew that he had hit it. He didn't know if he had killed the enemy soldier or not.

Carter leaped and almost yelled, "What in the hell are you doing?"

Rather than answer, he was on his feet, running again. He saw that Carter was behind him. He stopped, let her pass and then watched their trail for a moment. No one seemed interested in them any longer.

They came to the street and stopped. Carter flopped down, under the broadleaves of a bush. She was gasping for breath, panting quickly.

Tynan first checked their trail, but there was no movement along it. No more shadows dancing forward. Nothing. He turned and studied the street. There was no movement there either. Everyone had found cover.

Then behind him were several men shouting in Spanish. There were more shots. Single shots from AK-47s but nothing from the Americans and their M-16s.

Tynan slapped Carter on the shoulder and asked, "You ready now?"

"Yes."

"Then go. Straight across the street. Stop there."

She nodded and leaped to her feet. She ran forward, stumbled at the curb and fell to one knee. An instant later she was up and running again. Once she was across the street, Tynan followed. He hit the wall with his shoulder and slipped to the ground. Again he watched their trail, but there was no movement.

Tynan pointed to the left and Carter nodded. She began moving in that direction. After twenty or thirty yards, she stopped. Tynan saw that Hatcher was there, crouched in the shadows of a doorway.

"What's happening?" he hissed.

"Cubans," said Tynan. "You and Featherman okay?"

"Fine."

Tynan fell back into the darkness and wiped the sweat from his face. He pulled the magazine from his weapon and replaced it with a full one. He got to his knee and looked around quickly. From the distance, beyond the campus came more firing. AKs against old single shot rifles. A line of tracers arced into the sky.

A shape loomed out of the darkness and Blanchard plunged into the doorway. "Shit."

"Now what?" asked Hatcher.

"The smart move is to return to the raft and get the hell out," whispered Tynan.

"But we're not going to do that, are we?" asked Hatcher.

Tynan looked around and saw Carter crouched in the darkness. "Students are not at the university," he said. "No one's there but armed men."

"Right."

"Where are the students?"

She shrugged, realized that no one would be able to see that in the dark. "I couldn't begin to guess."

Hatcher said, "Depending on what they wanted to do, I'd say either the airport or the seaport."

"Maybe they'd take them downtown," said Featherman.

"No," said Tynan. "They'd either take them to a place where they'd be safer or to get them out of the country. That means we can check the airport since it's no more than two miles from here. If we have no luck there, we can check the port as we exfiltrate."

Hatcher took a deep breath and wiped the sweat from his face. "Odds are that they'll have been pulled out."

"I know that," said Tynan. He glanced at Carter. "What happened to that hotshot intelligence system? Why didn't someone tell us that the students had been moved?"

Carter said, "I don't know." But she did. One or two intell sources with only limited access to a radio net meant there was a lot that wasn't seen. No way the one or two men could see everything that everyone wanted them to see and even less that was reported. They had to focus on the important targets and ignore the minor ones.

"Do you think we're right? The airfield or the port?" asked Tynan.

"Makes some sense," she said. "Otherwise they could be anywhere in the city and we'd have no chance of finding them. Airport sounds as good as anything."

"She's a big help," hissed Blanchard.

"Okay," said Tynan. "I want Hatcher on point. Blanchard, you've got the rear. No more than ten or twelve yards behind us. To the airfield and we'll check that out. If we fail there, it's to the port for a survey. We have about five hours before we have to get to the sub. Questions?"

"How long do we search?"

"Depends on how long it takes us to get to the airfield and what we find there. Everyone ready?"

There were a couple of nods.

"Then let's do it."

Hatcher pulled out his map, checked it out and then said, "Here I go."

# 15

They reached the airport in less than an hour. They stayed to the darkened streets, dodging around burned out cars, a few scattered bodies, and the rubble of damaged buildings. Hatcher moved slowly at first, speeding up as they approached their destination. They scrambled across the streets, climbed a slight hill and came to a long, chain link fence. Hatcher crouched near the foot of it.

Tynan caught him there and saw the airfield spread out in front of him. There were almost no lights on it. Just a few places, where there were lanterns and a single hangar that had a band of dim light near the wall. A partially opened door revealed the interior lights.

"Shut down," said Hatcher.

"What'd you expect?"

"Thought the Cubans would have it open and operating so that they could get their soldiers and equipment in."

"During the day. During the night it's too bright. Draws in the enemy," said Tynan.

"Looks fairly deserted," whispered Hatcher. "Doesn't look like there is anyone around."

Tynan peeled the camouflage cover of his watch back

and checked the time. It was just after midnight. They had four hours to get back to the sub.

"Let's take a look quickly and then get the hell out of here," said Tynan.

"You don't think they're down there do you?" asked Hatcher quietly.

"No," said Tynan, "but we've got to go look. We'll split up into the same teams. One hour to look, fifteen minutes to get back here and then we'll get out."

Hatcher slipped back to where the others waited. Tynan joined Carter and the team split up again. Together the two officers slipped along the fence until they came to a place where someone had dug a hole to squeeze under. Tynan pointed and Carter nodded. She got down on her back and wiggled under the fence. Tynan followed her and in seconds they were on the same side of the fence.

She leaned close and asked, "Where to?"

Tynan pointed to the side of a building about fifty yards away. There were no lights near it and no evidence that anyone was guarding it. Now Tynan led the way, weaving right and left, using the cover available. They reached the building easily and stopped. Tynan noticed that the one door was riddled and the wall around it pockmarked. Tynan pointed at the bullet holes and shrapnel damage.

Carter looked at it and nodded her understanding.

Then, just as they had done at the campus, they slipped along the side of the building. They reached the tarmac, a huge paved area on the airfield side of the building. Tynan stretched out on the ground and tried to see something on the airfield. There were people moving about a hundred yards away, but they didn't seem to have a purpose. They were milling around rather than walking a post.

Tynan got up again and pressed his back against the wall. Using the building as cover, he stepped around and hurried along it until he came to a window. He peeked in the corner and saw that it was an office of some kind. Small and obviously uninhabited.

It was a fool's errand, he was sure. The students wouldn't be at the airfield because that would make it too simple. He was exposing his men for no reason. They had already run into the Cubans once and that had resulted in a firefight. He was tempted to call off the mission, but then decided to let it run its course for the time being.

He glanced to the left and saw that Carter was following him, just as she should be. Already she'd learned to control her breathing and she was moving over the concrete without making a sound.

It looked good for a moment, and then there was a sudden burst of firing at the far end of the airfield. A machine gun opened up, the ruby colored tracers of the heavy weapon bouncing over the ground and tumbling into the sky. The fight was a mile or more away, but close enough to alert everyone on the field. Then, suddenly, a flare burst overhead. Tynan froze, his shoulder against the wall. Carter dived for the ground like it was incoming mortars.

Slowly, Tynan turned his head. The field looked deserted, except for the machine gun firing. There was no rush to reinforce the machine gun nest. And just as quickly as it started, it ended. The flare sputtered, flashed and the parachute caught fire, dropping the flare to the ground.

"Let's go," said Tynan. He then sprinted across an open area between buildings, leaping for the shadows at the side of a hangar.

Carter followed and as she caught him, whispered, "What was that firing?"

"Who knows?" asked Tynan. "Forget it."

The radio clicked twice and Tynan pulled it out and raised the antenna. "This is Diamond One."

"This is Diamond Three. We've reached the far end of the field and found no evidence of the students."

"Roger. Diamond Two, say location."

"This is Two. We're just south of the main runway, working our way across."

"Roger." Tynan telescoped the antenna and put the radio away. He glanced at Carter, but didn't say a word to her. He moved forward, along the side of the building.

Carter stayed close to him. There seemed to be no one around them. In the distance was noise, and there were guards on one of the hangars. Tynan pointed at them and Carter nodded.

"If the students are here, that's where they'll be."

Leaning close, she asked, "What are you going to do?"

"Check it out. If they're not there, we'll get out, following this path to the rear."

She nodded but didn't speak.

Tynan slipped along the building, keeping his eyes moving and listening for noise. At the edge of the hangar he stopped but there was no movement between it and the next building. He ran across the open ground and dropped down behind a pile of crates. He watched Carter follow him and once she had caught him, he was up and moving again.

As he rounded a corner, he stopped dead in his tracks. A Cuban stood there, a cigarette in his hand. The soldier looked at Tynan and in Spanish asked, "Who are you?"

There was nothing Tynan could do. The man had seen him. Spoken to him. He struck at once. A punch to the man's stomach and a chop to the neck. He heard the fragile bones snap as the man dropped to the ground. There was a quiet groan, and then silence.

With the toe of his boot, Tynan crushed the glowing tip of the cigarette. He then crouched and felt for the pulse.

The man was dead. Irrationally, Tynan realized that smoking was bad for your health. It would kill you. He forced the thought from his mind and dragged the body to the rear.

"What the hell?" asked Carter.

Tynan shot her a look and said, "Keep your voice down."

They rolled the body out of sight. Tynan took the man's weapon, stripped the bolt from it and put it in his pocket. The Cubans could replace the bolt later, but at the moment, the weapon was inoperative.

Again he started toward the front of the hangar, but Carter stopped him. "Be careful," she said.

Tynan nodded but didn't speak. That was the problem with amateurs. They always felt the need to speak and question. There was no reason for her to have spoken. Everything was obvious. Tynan shoved that thought aside too, and began to work his way around the front of the hangar.

This time he made it easily. There were no more men out there smoking. In fact there were no guards at all, which worried him. The Cubans were on a hostile airfield, surrounded by unhappy local citizens, and they didn't seem to be taking their situation seriously. Tynan and his men had penetrated the airfield easily, without trouble.

The next destination was the hangar where there was some light. Tynan looked at the side of it, away from the airfield. He studied it, looking for a sign of life, but couldn't spot anything. That was the thing about guards, almost everyone always had the guards moving, walking a post. Maybe they thought it kept the guards awake on those long tours of duty, but all it did was make them easy targets for attackers. Movement was the fastest way to be spotted. A stationary guard, concealed, would be more effective.

Tynan turned and saw that Carter was right behind him, her pistol in her hand. He leaned close and said, "You wait until I'm across the open ground. Wait until you see me disappear. Then you follow. Anything goes wrong, you get out."

She nodded her understanding.

With that, Tynan took off. He ran straight across the open ground, trying to stay in the shadows. He reached the other side and dived into a shadow and faced toward the front. There was no sign that anyone saw him.

He stayed there, glancing to the left where Carter was. A moment later, she ran from the edge of the building, coming directly at him. She got there, dropped to her knees and then leaned forward, breathing hard. Sill there was no sign that anyone knew they were out there.

Tynan got to his feet and moved along the side of the hangar, toward a group of windows. He peeked in, saw nothing and ducked down. He moved forward another twenty feet and looked in another window. There was a dim light filtering in a partially closed door. There was enough light to illuminate the interior of the office, showing him that it was deserted.

Moving again, he came to another group of windows but there was nothing to see through them. The doors were closed and there was no movement.

Turning, he waved Carter forward, pointing at his feet. He didn't know if she'd understand that he wanted her to move right to that point and stop.

As she got up to move, Tynan did the same, heading to the front of the hangar. He hesitated at the corner, looked around it and saw that the tarmac was deserted. A dim light bled out the hangar door, showing him more of the area.

From the interior came the sound of voices. One or two

people talking quietly. He couldn't make out the words but thought it sounded like English.

Glancing to the rear, he saw that Carter had understood the instruction. She had stopped right where he wanted her. He gave her the same instruction, and as she began to work her way forward, Tynan slipped around the corner. He crouched, moving carefully, silently until he came to a small door set into the larger hangar door.

Peeking through the dirty glass, he could now see the interior of the hangar. There was some military equipment close to him. An armored personnel carrier and a jeep. A couple of soldiers were standing around it and two were on the floor in sleeping bags.

Beyond them though, scattered in the center of the hangar, were civilians. Fifty or sixty of them, men and women. He ducked back and closed his eyes, concentrating on what he had just seen. He reviewed it all and then nodded. He popped up again, looked through the window and then retreated, moving to the corner where Carter waited.

"I think I've found them," he whispered.

"You sure?"

Tynan didn't answer that question. He got out his radio and pulled up the antenna. Into it he whispered, "Diamond Two, Diamond Three, I have located the bundle. Northern end of the field, in the hangar with the light. Acknowledge."

There were two quick bursts as one team hit the mike button twice. That was followed by two more. Both teams rogering the call.

"Now what?" asked Carter.

Tynan looked at her and wished she'd just be quiet. Leaning close, he said, "We wait."

He moved around her, ducking back, deeper into the

shadows. Tynan was up against the wall so that he could watch what was going on in front of him.

Carter touched his shoulder and leaned close to his ear. "You sure it was the American students?"

Tynan shrugged but didn't answer. All he'd seen were a group of civilians in the center of the hangar. They didn't look like locals, but then they could have been Cuban civilians on the island for some reason. But they didn't look Cuban either. They'd have to wait to find out.

It was then that the first faint sounds of the aircraft engines could be heard. Tynan glanced to the north, but couldn't see the aircraft. He peeled back the camouflage band on his watch and saw that it was nearing zero one hundred. It didn't make sense for the Cubans to bring in equipment that late at night, unless they were hoping to sneak it in while the locals were asleep.

The aircraft engines grew louder and still there were no signs of lights on the plane or along the runways. But there was sudden activity on the field. Men were pouring out of one of the hangars, running across the taxiways. A group of them stopped at the intersection of a runway and a taxiway. They pulled a tarp off an anti-aircraft gun and spun it around until it was aimed to the north.

Tynan turned and now could see the aircraft above them. A distant plane barely visible in the dark. A high wing craft with four turbo props that looked like an American made C-130 Hercules.

Apparently the Cubans had it spotted too. There was a quick burst from one of the anti-aircraft guns. Red tracers floating up, toward the aircraft.

"Shit!" said Tynan. He ran forward, toward the edge of the hangar and knelt there. The plane kept coming, the roar of the engines louder.

Tynan aimed his weapon at the anti-aircraft gun. He

hesitated, but the gun began to fire again. Short bursts, aimed at the incoming plane. Tynan returned the fire. A quick burst and then a longer one. He burned through the magazine. The last three rounds streaked out. Tracers that told him the magazine was coming up on empty.

He reloaded as Carter yelled, "What's happening?"

He waved an arm at her. "Cover me! Watch my back."

She moved around and crouched behind him, staring into the blackness at the rear of the hangar.

The firing at the anti-aircraft increased. A hundred rounds danced skyward. The ruby colored tracers seemed to float up, toward the plane.

Again Tynan fired, this time in short bursts. He watched for signs that he was doing good. Sparks flew as one round hit the protective plate in front of the machine gun and ricochetted.

Then firing broke out from another of the buildings. More rounds aimed at the anti-aircraft weapon. Bullets kicking up dirt, whining off the concrete and tumbling through the air. The machine gun then fell silent. Tynan saw one of the Cubans abandon his position, running toward him. A bullet caught the man in the back, lifted him and threw him to the ground.

A second battery at the far end of the field opened fire. It was joined by a second and then a third. The hammering of the weapons ripped the night to shreds. The tracers streamed into the sky, but the single C-130 came on.

Tynan glanced at Carter and ordered, "You wait right here. Don't move." He took off then, running across the field, toward the abandoned anti-aircraft weapon. He reached it, leaped into the seat used by the gunner and cranked it around. Using another wheel, he lowered the barrel until it was level with the ground. Then, aiming at the second of the anti-aircraft positions, he opened fire.

Short burst. Four, five, six rounds. One tracer for every regular round. Firing and waiting and firing again, as the aircraft passed over his head.

Bullets began to strike the weapon and the ground around him. They snapped overhead, sounding like bees zipping past. He ignored them, firing on the other weapons.

And then the C-130 was over them, flying on, toward the south. The enemy gunners followed it, firing up at it as Tynan shot at them.

Moments later, parachutes appeared behind the plane. Troops assaulting the island. The Cubans kept shooting, now trying to kill the men on the chutes.

A shape moved from one of the hangars, running at the closest of the anti-aircraft guns. The man was firing, trying to kill the gunners. He stopped once, throwing himself prone and squeezed off a sustained burst. Two Cuban gunners fell and the third gave up, running away.

Tynan shifted around, taking the last of the Cuban held weapons under fire. He put a dozen bursts into it. Tracers hit it and bounced high, tumbling. The firing there ended as the Cubans suddenly fled.

The last of the firing stopped and the sound of the transport's engines faded. Tynan slowly stood up, getting off the anti-aircraft weapon. He saw the shape that had attacked the other machine gun start toward him, carrying an M-16. He crouched down, ready, but then Hatcher loomed out of the darkness and asked, "What in the fuck is going on here?"

Tynan shrugged. He didn't have a clue.

# 16

The first burst of firing didn't surprise Salinas. He knew that the gun crews sometimes cleared their weapons with short bursts to break up the boredom. But then came other firing. Sustained bursts from the anti-aircraft and from assault rifles. And the roaring of aircraft engines.

Salinas, in a small office tucked in the rear of a hangar, leaped up then. He grabbed his pistol belt and ran to the door. He saw his men hurrying toward the front of the hangar. Quickly buckling his pistol belt, he joined them. He spotted a sergeant and yelled, "What is going on?"

The sergeant glanced to the rear and said, "I don't know, sir. Firing outside."

The men scattered then, working their way toward the doors. Overhead was the roar of a transport plane. As they watched, the aircraft began to drop paratroopers south of the field. The anti-aircraft began to hammer again then, the rounds drifted up at the men falling from the aircraft.

"Sergeant," yelled Salinas. "Get your men organized. Prepare to reinforce the guards on the south side of the field."

"Yes sir." The man whirled and shouted, "Fall in now. Let's go."

Salinas pulled back, away from the door. He ran across the hangar floor and found one of his officers. "We have paratroopers landing in the south."

"Yes sir."

"Take the men out the side, use the hangar for cover. And hurry."

There was more shooting from the airfield. Three of the batteries firing. Salinas looked out a window and saw that one of the batteries was firing along the ground. He didn't understand that, but as he watched, the gun stopped firing. All three batteries fell silent then.

The men were running back across the hangar floor and filtering out, through a side door. Salinas watched them and then thought of the students in one of the other buildings. He needed to get to them and see what they were doing.

He ran back to his room and grabbed a shirt. As he put it on, he ran out, listening for sounds outside, but nothing was going on. At the door, he slipped to a stop and saw some of his men running from the anti-aircraft batteries. He stepped out and shouted, "Return to your posts, immediately."

One of the men halted at the edge of the tarmac and then knelt. Salinas saw him raise his weapon and knew the man was going to fire. Salinas dived for cover, found himself lying in the open on the tarmac as the rifleman opened up. Three or four shots that passed over his head. Salinas rolled to the right and the man got up and ran.

As that man disappeared, Salinas was up on his feet, returning to the hangar. There were a couple of men in it and he shouted at them. "Come with me. Now."

They ran to the front of the hangar and hesitated for a moment. Firing had broken out on the southern end of the airfield, but it didn't seem to be much of a firefight.

Blanchard had watched as the anti-aircraft guns had shot it out with one another. As the paratroopers jumped, he figured that Tynan or Hatcher had captured one of the enemy weapons and had turned it on the others. There was no reason for him to try to do that. They had it all under control. The fight was going to develop on the southern side of the airfield and that's where he wanted to be.

He tapped Smith on the arm and pointed toward the south. He took off running, toward the fence. He ducked low, saw a depression in the ground and dived for cover there. Smith joined him, his weapon pointed out, toward the enemy.

"Don't fire yet," said Blanchard. "Let's make sure of the targets."

Firing from the anti-aircraft guns had faded and the aircraft that had dropped the soldiers was long gone. There was no sound and no movement from the open ground south of the airfield, but Blanchard knew that the men there were getting organized to move on the field. Americans, obviously, with orders to take the field.

Then suddenly, from the north came the sound of men running. Blanchard shifted around and saw the shadows of the Cubans as they hurried forward. A mass of them, maybe as many as forty. All armed with AKs.

"Okay," said Blanchard. "Now we earn our money."

Smith saw the Cubans and nodded.

"On three we both open fire on full auto. Burn through the magazine. Hold the trigger down. And aim low. Aim for the knees."

"I'm shooting to kill," said Smith.

"Me too," said Blanchard. "If you consciously aim at the knees at night, you usually put the rounds into them chest high. On three now."

"Go!"

Blanchard flipped off the safety and said, "One. Two. Three." On three, he pulled the trigger, holding it back as the M-16 burned through the whole magazine. He lost sight of the enemy in the muzzle flash of his own weapon. He heard the ejected shells hitting the ground and felt those thrown out by Smith's weapon hitting him.

As soon as the bolt locked back, he whipped out a second magazine. He jammed it home, slapped the bottom and worked the bolt, stripping the first round into the chamber. Now he looked toward the enemy soldiers. They had scattered, running for cover. Half a dozen of them lay on the ground.

"Okay, hold your fire," he said.

Smith ducked down then.

The Cubans opened fire, a couple of rounds snapping overhead. Then the ground around him seemed to come alive. It danced and splashed as the enemy tried to kill him. Ducking down, he felt the flying stones sting his bare skin.

Firing from the Cubans slowed and then stopped. Blanchard said, "We'll give them another magazine. Right. NOW!"

He popped up and opened fire. The ground around him seemed to erupt, but he ignored it, shooting at the running figures. He kept both eyes open and swung the barrel. In front of him, the enemy seemed to flash and sparkle as they fired at him. Aiming at the center of the muzzle flashes, he saw one soldier and then another fall.

But this time they didn't scramble for cover. They kept

running at him, firing from the hips. A dozen of them, screaming at him, the words lost in the noise.

"Here they come!" screamed Smith.

"Take them down! Take them down."

Blanchard's weapon was suddenly empty again. "Reloading," he shouted as he pulled the magazine free and tossed it aside. "Ready," he said as he jammed the fully loaded magazine home and worked the bolt.

Now the Cubans were no more than a dozen yards away, firing directly at them. The ground around them shook under the impact of AK rounds. Dust hung in the air along with the smoke of gunpowder. Blanchard was screaming at the onrushing enemy, daring them to come at him.

"Reloading," yelled Smith. He tried to make it quick and smooth but his fingers were suddenly sausage sized with no feeling in them. He fumbled at the magazine release and then had trouble getting a loaded magazine from his pouch.

"Hurry," demanded Blanchard. He was now firing on single shot, trying to knock down the Cubans.

Smith worked the bolt and stuck the barrel of his weapon over the lip of the depression. He pulled the trigger and heard the shriek of a wounded soldier.

But then the Cubans were on them, screaming and thrusting with bayonets. Smith felt the white cold pain as a bayonet cut his arm. He rolled left, to his back and aimed up, at the man standing over him. As the Cubans attacked, Smith fired once, twice and felt steaming hot blood splash his face as the soldier flipped back away from him.

Next to Smith, Blanchard was on his feet. A Cuban soldier thrust with his bayonet. Blanchard countered with his weapon, tossed it aside and grabbed the barrel of the AK. He fell to the rear, dragging the Cuban with him. As they dropped, Blanchard stuck out a foot, shoved it into the midriff of the enemy and kicked him over to his back. As the soldier fell, Blanchard ripped the AK from his hands. He whirled and fired, putting two rounds into the Cuban's chest.

Smith burned through the last magazine and then threw away his M-16. He drew his pistol and fired as fast as he could point and aim. Seven quick shots as the Cubans reached him. One man was hit in the shoulder and rolled away. Another took a bullet in the sternum and fell at Smith's feet.

But suddenly there were too many of them. He felt someone grab his arm and he tried to turn the weapon on him and failed. There was a sudden pain in his side. He fell to the rear and one man fell on top of him. Smith dropped his pistol and tried to get to his knife. He twisted once and slammed a fist into the face of the Cuban soldier. He could hear the breath rasping in the enemy's throat and smell the odor of his last meal.

The knife came free and Smith struck with it. There was a sound like tires on dry concrete. The man stiffened and died and the air was filled with the stench of bowel.

Smith threw the body off and tried to roll clear. The ground around him exploded as another Cuban tried to shoot him. The muzzle flash almost touched him. There were sudden explosions of white hot pain. Smith didn't understand that his luck had run out.

Blanchard, next to him was having more luck. He emptied the AK into the oncoming enemy soldiers and then used the bayonet. He parried a single thrust, came around with the butt and felt the weapon strike bone. The Cuban dropped away and there was another standing there. Blanchard used the bayonet, driving it into the throat of the enemy. The man screamed and fell.

Now there were others. They came at him firing quickly. Blanchard knew then it was all over. He had seen Smith die. No one to cover him as he reloaded. Too many of them coming at him, shooting at him.

A round hit him high, spinning him. He threw the AK away as he fell face first into the soft dirt. There was no pain. A throbbing in his shoulder that was in time to his heart beat. There was a wetness under him and he knew that he was bleeding badly. If the Cubans would run off, he might be able to stop the flow of blood.

But the Cubans didn't run off. They swept into the depression, trying to help their wounded fellows and to make sure that the two enemy soldiers were dead. Blanchard heard them fire a round into Smith's head. A single bullet to make sure that Smith would not suddenly surprise them. Blanchard knew that he was next but didn't have the energy, didn't have the strength to move or to fight. He knew he was about to die and couldn't even find the strength to be frightened about that.

As his blood pumped from the wound in his shoulder, he heard the Cuban cock his pistol. The sound was unnaturally loud. He heard the Cuban say, in accented English, "You die, pig."

He never heard the shot fired.

Tynan watched as the firefight began at the south end of the airfield and was afraid that it was Blanchard and Smith. He didn't think the paratroopers had had enough time to get to the airfield. Blanchard and Smith were going to be in trouble, but there wasn't much he could do for them except hope they could get themselves out of the situation.

"Lieutenant?" asked Hatcher.

"Come on," he said.

They raced across the tarmac and reached the hangar without being shot at. Tynan flattened himself against the wall and slipped along it. Hatcher was right next to him.

They stopped next to a small door and Tynan reached up and grabbed the knob. The noise of the firefight covered any sound that he might make and the flashing of the weapons would draw the enemy's attention.

Tynan hesitated for a moment, saw that Hatcher was ready and noticed that Carter had joined them. He'd told her to cover their back, but now she was right there with them. Featherman was on the other side of the hangar, lying in the shadows, covering them.

"Ready?" he asked.

"Go," said Hatcher.

Tynan opened the door then, jerking it wide. As he did, Hatcher dived through. Tynan followed him, rolled and came up on his knee. A Cuban was running at them from the left. Hatcher was up, ready to meet the threat.

Hatcher swung a fist and knocked the Cuban off his feet. He kicked him once, snapping the soldier's head back. There was a groan from the man as he collapsed.

With that both men were up and running. They crossed part of the floor when someone fired a single shot at them. Tynan dived to the right and rolled, turning so that he could look for the sniper.

Someone screamed and the students were suddenly in turmoil. Hatcher continued to run at them. "American soldiers. We're American soldiers."

Tynan came up on his knees. He saw a Cuban in the catwalks above them. He aimed, fired, missed and fired again. The Cuban returned the fire, the AK round ricochetted off the floor near his knee.

"Get down," ordered Hatcher. "Get down."

But the students weren't listening. Men and women were running and screaming. One or two of them had hit the floor. They were in turmoil.

Tynan fired again and the Cuban dropped his weapon over the railing. He fell back, onto the catwalk and didn't move. Tynan whirled and saw another Cuban standing in the doorway of one of the offices. He wasn't doing anything, except standing there. Tynan fired at him. The round hit the door, seeming to awaken the man. He dived for cover.

There were shouts, screams and firing from outside. From somewhere else.

"American soldiers," yelled Hatcher again and again, but the students were paying no attention to him. They were on the floor, hands protecting their heads, hoping to survive the fight.

Carter ran into the hangar then. She still carried the pistol that she had yet to fire. Tynan ran toward the group that was beginning to quiet down.

"Everyone," he shouted. "I'm an American Naval officer sent here to get you out. Please, everyone, settle down."

Carter ran up to Tynan and stopped near him. "There's someone coming," she shouted.

Tynan looked at the men and women and then aimed at the ceiling of the hangar. He fired a burst into it. A dozen shots that overpowered the noise being made. Suddenly there was silence in the hangar. Everyone was staring at him.

"I'm an American Naval officer," he repeated. "Sent here to get you out."

There was an instant of silence and then suddenly, wild cheering. The students were up, off the floor running toward him, slapping him on the back and wanting to shake his hand. They were shouting questions at him.

There was firing from outside. Closer. Hatcher whirled and looked at Tynan. "Got to be Featherman."

"Go. Get him out."

Hatcher nodded and took off, running across the hangar floor. He slid to a halt and dropped to a prone position. He crawled forward rapidly.

"Jillian," shouted Tynan. "Take charge here and get them out. To the rear of the hangar and to the road. You know where to take them."

"What about you?"

"We'll cover the withdrawal and join you then."

She stared at him, almost as if afraid to move. Then, suddenly she nodded and shouted, "Everyone, follow me. Let's get out of here."

Tynan watched as she ran toward the rear of the hangar and a small door there. The students fell in behind her, following her just as the children of Hamlin had followed the Pied Piper.

As that happened, Tynan turned and ran to the front of the hangar. He reached the door they had used to enter and saw that Cubans were running toward them. Not a full attack, yet, but a probe to see what they were doing and how strong they were.

Tynan took a deep breath and opened fire. Two, three rounds at the running men. One of them fell. Firing broke out from them. Shots fired from the hip.

Hatcher opened up on full auto. He burned through a magazine and then rolled to the right, behind the thick hangar door. The Cubans fired at him. The rounds slammed into the metal shaking it. Paint chips flaked off, raining down like the leaves of an autumn oak.

"Get Featherman in here," shouted Tynan.

Hatcher repeated the message and the firing outside increased. Tynan returned it and Featherman sprinted into the open hangar door, diving and rolling over, head over heels. He glanced at Tynan, not far away from him and grinned sheepishly.

Tynan nodded and then shouted, "Let's get out of here. Now." He was up then, moving to the rear. Hatcher and Featherman were doing the same thing. From the outside came sporadic firing as if the Cubans weren't sure what was happening.

Tynan didn't wait for them to figure it out. He sprinted across the floor to follow Carter and the students. Hatcher and Featherman were close behind him.

## 17

Salinas watched the firefight at the south end of the airfield until it was over. One of his men ran back to him, slid to a halt near him and then, gasping for breath, said, "American soldiers. They're dead."

"You're sure they're Americans?"

The man shrugged. That had been everyone's assumption and he had reported it. Now he wasn't sure.

"It's not important," snapped Salinas. "I want the bodies preserved now. Bring them back here."

"Yes sir." The man whirled and ran off.

Firing broke out to the left, toward the eastern end of the field. Salinas dived to the rear and then looked. Suddenly it was all clear to him. The fighting in the south had been a diversion. Salinas leaped up and ran into the hangar. He found a squad of men there, crouched near the windows, watching the show to the south.

"You men come with me," he ordered. Without waiting for a response, he whirled and ran for the door.

There, he halted and knelt. He pulled his pistol from his holster and thumbed back the hammer. He glanced over his shoulder, saw that the squad was crowded near him and said, "Let's go."

Outside, they ran across the tarmac, toward the hangar where the students were being held. Halfway to it, they were shot at. Two, three rounds snapping overhead. Salinas sprawled to the ground and fired in return. The squad knelt near him, firing into the darkness.

A single shape suddenly jumped up and ran for the hangar door. Firing poured from it, pinning them down. They returned it, but the firing from the hangar tapered and died. Fearing a trick, they stayed where they were, but the invaders in the hangar didn't shoot again.

With his patience running out, Salinas jumped up and waved his arm. "Follow me," he ordered.

Again he was running for the hangar, shouting. He squeezed off a shot by accident, and then reached the corner of the building. There he stopped to catch his breath. He didn't care that the students were in there and could be caught in the crossfire. If that happened, the invaders would be blamed. It was their fault, not his.

With the men grouped around him, he knew it was time. He checked his pistol and then launched himself around the corner. Through the open door, he saw the fleeing figures of three armed men. The students were gone and two of his men lay sprawled on the hangar floor.

Salinas opened fire. He emptied his pistol and then ducked back as the rest of his squad flowed around him, using their assault rifles. The sound of the firing was reflected and amplified by the hangar walls. In seconds it seemed that a thousand men were firing at one another.

The running men, at the sound of the first sounds, dived for cover. They returned the fire, first slowing and then on full automatic, driving the Cubans back, away from the hangar door.

Having reloaded, Salinas was ready to attack again. He peeked up, through the glass set in the small door. It shattered suddenly, spraying him with razor sharp shards. He felt them rip at his face and his uniform. He fell back, the blood wet on his face.

He looked at his men then and ordered, "Kill them. Kill them all."

The first shots had been wild. Tynan didn't pay much attention to them until he reached the far end of the hangar. Once there, he searched for refuge among the equipment and boxes stored there. He found cover, spun and fired a quick burst.

Hatcher and Featherman did the same. As they found safety at the far end of the hangar, they began to shoot at the Cuban soldiers, driving them from the building.

As the shooting ebbed, Tynan whipped out his radio, extended the antenna and said, rapidly, "Diamond Three, Diamond Three, this is Diamond One. Get out now."

Firing came again. A dozen weapons on full auto. Tynan dropped the radio to the concrete floor and spun. He fired twice on single shot and then flipped the selector to full auto.

Men were running toward him, coming around the open doors of the hangar. Small, dark men in green uniforms and carrying the Russian made AK-47. Men who were shouting, screaming, firing as they ran toward Tynan, trying to frighten him with the noise.

Almost calmly, Tynan squeezed the trigger, firing a short burst. One man took the rounds in the crotch and the stomach. His forward momentum carried him on until he fell, sliding on the smooth floor of the hangar. Blood flowed from half a dozen wounds.

Rounds were slamming into the area around Tynan. Chips of concrete were kicked up. Splinters of wood ripped from the packing crates. The noise was deafening.

Hatcher was firing single shot, picking his targets as if he was on the range and the enemy was nothing more than dark green cutouts. He aimed at those closest, fired and fired and fired until the man went down. One of them spun and lost his rifle. A second came off his feet as if he had run into an invisible barricade. It was one, two, three, for Hatcher.

Featherman was not as calm as the two veterans. He saw the enemy running at him, screaming at him, trying to kill him, and he wanted to stop them. Now. Immediately. He was firing on full automatic, spraying the rounds like a fireman with a hose. He was trying to kill everyone at once.

When his weapon was empty, he dropped down, his back against a packing crate, his head nearly on the floor. He struggled with the rifle, trying to get the empty magazine out and the loaded one in, but everything seemed to move in slow motion. No matter how he hurried, it seemed that hours were passing.

Finally, ready, he whirled and fired without aiming. One of the Cubans was halfway cross the floor, coming right at him. As if in a dream, Featherman aimed. He knew the shot was good. He could almost see the blood splatter, but the soldier didn't fall. He didn't even stumble. It was as if he didn't feel the bullet stinging his flesh. He came on, running straight for Featherman, screaming.

Now the young soldier was in a panic, convinced his weapon was no good. And yet he continued to fire. He jerked the trigger down, holding it, his aim on the single Cuban who seemed invincible. He ignored everything else.

And then the man seemed to be lifted from his feet and thrown to her rear. He landed on his back and skidded a few feet to lie still. His weapon was clutched in his hand, but he didn't use it.

But Featherman's attention had been on that one man to
the exclusion of everyone else. As he turned, he saw a
Cuban soldier drawing a bead on him. Featherman
screamed in surprise and rolled to the left swinging his
weapon around. The Cuban fired and Featherman was sure
that he missed. Featherman pulled his trigger. There was a
short burst and the bolt locked back.

The Cuban had been hit once. A round that hit the point
of his shoulder, deadening his right arm and hand. Blood
poured from the wound as he wobbled on his now unsteady
feet. He shifted the AK from his right hand to his left,
holding it like it was a pistol.

Featherman struggled to pull his own pistol. As it
cleared the holster, the Cuban fired again. The bullets hit
all around Featherman. One of them stung his leg and another hit his chest. But he fired his pistol, pulling the trigger twice before the weapon was too heavy to hold. It fell
from his fingers.

Hatcher saw the Cuban out of the corner of his eye. He
dived and rolled and fired twice as the enemy soldier
dropped. He fired a final time and the Cuban soldier was
dead.

Tynan kept pouring out rounds. Single shots and short
bursts. Four or five quick rounds. At the far end of the
hangar, he saw a Cuban officer enter. One man bringing up
the rear, waving his pistol as if he wanted attention.

Tynan aimed at the man and pulled the trigger slowly.

Salinas reloaded as his men ran into the hangar and the
battle started for real. Everyone firing as fast as he could.
Salinas crouched at the entrance and watched. A couple of
his men fell and then more as they spread out across the
floor. Salinas fired at the Americans hidden at the far end.
No one seemed to know that he was there.

He emptied his pistol, reloaded and decided it was time to join the assault. He ran around the corner of the door and stopped once to snap off a single shot.

As he started forward, he saw the tall American at the far end of the hangar aim at him. Their eyes seemed to lock and in that instance, Salinas knew that he had made a mistake. He was about to die and there was nothing he could do about it. He froze then, unable to act.

The first round punched through his belly, exploding out his back and he felt nothing from it. A pinprick of heat. And a dampness that crawled down his back.

The second round knocked him from his feet. He was suddenly staring up into the dark regions of the hangar, where there were hanging lights and cables and a confusion of crosswalks and beams to brace the building. A fascinating sight that he'd never seen because he'd never bothered to look up.

And then it all faded from sight. There was noise around him. Shouting and shooting and cries of pain from the wounded. There were a few commands. And then there was silence as he lost consciousness and his blood continued to pump out of him quickly.

As the Cuban leader died, Tynan turned his attention on the other soldiers. Now there were only a few of them left standing and they were no longer interested in attacking. They were scrambling right and left, trying to get out of the line of fire. One man dived through a doorway as the frame exploded in a hail of bullets. Hatcher had missed him.

The firing tapered and then was sporadic. Tynan picked up the radio and then glanced over at Hatcher. "Where's Featherman?" he demanded.

Hatcher looked at the body. There was a large pool of

blood around it so that it looked as if it was floating. Featherman's face was white, waxy looking. Hatcher knew that he hadn't survived the attack.

"He's dead."

Tynan nodded and then used the radio. "Diamond Three, Diamond Three, this is One. Say status."

There was no return message. Nothing.

Tynan keyed the mike and repeated his message and then added, "Fall back now. Escape and evade at the first opportunity."

Hatcher moved closer to Tynan. "What are we going to do now?"

"Get the hell out."

"What about Featherman?"

"We'll have to leave the body. Nothing we can do about that. But I'm not going to risk my life to save a dead man."

"What about his teeth?" asked Hatcher.

Tynan understood the question. Here was an American serviceman, killed on foreign soil. It could be embarrassing to have the body identified, and yet it seemed that more Americans were being landed. No one was going to worry about an additional American serviceman. It wasn't as if the mission was completely covert.

"Don't worry about them," he said. "You see anything of Blanchard and Smith?"

"South end of the field."

Tynan collapsed the antenna. He peeked over the cartons and equipment. There was a haze hanging in the air created by the gunfire. Smoke and dust from the battle. There were a dozen bodies lying on the floor. Most of them ripped apart by the M-16 rounds. Blood stood in pools. Some of the wounded were moaning quietly. The survivors had found cover in the offices or outside the hangar and none of them were inclined to attack again.

"Let's get out of here now," said Tynan.

"Go ahead, sir. I'll cover."

Tynan nodded. He checked his weapon, made sure that he had a fully loaded magazine and then crawled to the rear. He reached up for the knob of the small door, twisted it and pushed. As the door swung open, he dived out.

He was surprised how fresh and cool the air seemed outside. The acrid stink of the cordite that had stung his lungs and his nose was gone. The heat generated by the fighting was gone. Cool and fresh.

He stayed there, covering as Hatcher joined him. He crouched in the doorway and took a final look.

Tynan slapped his shoulder and said, "Let's find Carter and get the hell out of here."

"Right."

The two of them took off running, first up the slight hill behind the hangar and then down toward the road. Tynan hoped they would find Carter quickly.

# 18

Carter and the students were moving rapidly, staying on the road. She had divided them into two groups, one on each shoulder so that they were walking along just like the soldiers in a World War II epic. They were hurrying forward without much talking or discussion. They believed what Carter had told them. The Cubans were holding them for unknown reasons, and she, along with the others had been sent to escort them off the island. Had they had the chance, they would have cheered. Instead they rushed out the rear of the hangar, up the slight hill and then down to the road. Carter organized two groups and had them moving rapidly.

That done, she ranged up and down the line, urging the men and women to hurry up, to keep quiet, and to help one another. She kept them moving silently, headed for the port facility.

The small radio she had crackled to life. The voice was muffled, impossible to hear. She stopped moving, jerked the radio from her pocket and yanked at the antenna.

"Diamond One Alpha, this is Diamond One. Say location."

She glanced around, saw that they were inside the city, heading toward the port. She reported that.

"Roger. We are following. Plan to rendezvous in one five minutes."

"Understood." She waited and when there was nothing more, she collapsed the antenna and put the radio away.

She hurried to the head of the short column and stopped at a cross street. She glanced right and left and then hurried across it. There was heavy firing now to the south and she was sure that the American paratroopers were fighting with the Cubans. It wasn't her concern, as long as they stayed to the south.

She ran down the block, to the next street, saw nothing and turned to retreat.

"Alto!" yelled someone.

Carter froze. She held her pistol in one hand, but apparently her body concealed it from the soldier behind her. She glanced over her shoulder, at the shape that was moving from the darkness of a doorway.

In Spanish, the man ordered her to turn around completely. She saw that he was armed with an AK and that it was pointed, more or less, in her direction.

The idea came to her in the middle of a thought. An idea born of Saturday afternoons in the movies where the hero always spins and fires once, surprising the nefarious enemy. A simple trick that never failed in the movies.

Carter spun suddenly, lifted her weapon and squeezed the trigger. The pistol boomed and the flame shot from the barrel as the weapon bucked and twisted in her hand. The bullet hit stone and bounced off screaming.

The Cuban responded quickly firing his assault rifle. Bullets hit the pavement near her feet and then snapped by her ears as he recovered. The muzzle flash stabbed out reaching for her.

Unconsciously she lifed one foot to protect it. She wrapped her arm around her head and held out the pistol, pulling the trigger again and again. The booming filled the streets and reflected from the walls. She kept firing until the weapon was empty.

And when she looked, the Cuban soldier was lying in the street. One of the students ran forward and grabbed the weapon from the dead man. He tugged at the ammo pouch, couldn't get it, and settled for taking a spare magazine out of it.

"Leave it," ordered Carter.

"No way," said the man.

"They catch us and you can be shot if you have a weapon. You're safer without it."

"No." He stood up to face her.

"Alto!" yelled another voice.

"Christ," said Carter. She knelt fumbling with the pistol as the student opened fire.

The Cuban who had yelled jumped into a doorway and shot back. One burst that slammed into a building near them.

Carter managed to drop the empty magazine from her weapon. As she tried to fit the other one in, she yelled, "Run! Toward the ocean! Everyone run!"

The student with the AK leaped across the street and used the corner of the building for protection. Carter got her weapon loaded and worked the slide, chambering a round. The Cuban stepped into the street and Carter fired at him. She dropped to one knee and held the pistol at arm's length, trying to aim it, but it was too dark in the street. She just kept shooting until the enemy fell to his side.

Then she was up and running after the students. She got out of the intersection and leaned back against the building. Sweat soaked her uniform and her breath was coming in gasps. It was as if she had run a hundred yards, a hundred miles. Her hands were sweat slick and she fumbled the radio as she tried to get it out.

Suddenly, before she could make a call, Tynan was there, his face only inches from hers. "You okay?" he asked.

"Yes."

"The students?"

She pointed down the street. "Running for the ocean."

"Hatcher, catch them and escort them."

"Yes sir."

As the Army sergeant ran off, Tynan moved back to the corner of the building. In the shadows of the street, he could see the bodies of the two Cuban soldiers, but there was no movement around them. A two man roveing patrol that had walked into a buzz saw named Carter.

He returned to her. "You okay?" he asked again.

"I'm fine. Why do you keep asking?"

He ignored that and said, "Then let's go. I'll follow you now."

Carter took off in a slow trot, keeping close to the building as they had done when they moved into the town. They kept the pace steady. Tynan halted at each of the cross streets, but there were no signs of the Cubans. Firing in the south with tracers lancing upwards, into the night sky, but no sign of the soldiers advancing on them.

They caught the rear of the student formation. Hatcher had them lined up on both sides of the street, crouching in the shadows at the foot of the buildings. Tynan ordered Carter to stay where she was and guard the rear of the formation.

"You see anything you can't identify, open fire."

"But what if it's more of our people?"

"All you're doing is alerting Hatcher and me that there's a problem back here."

"Oh."

Tynan turned and ran toward Hatcher. He dropped to the sidewalk next to the sergeant. "What you got here?"

Hatcher wiped at the sweat on his face, smearing the camo paint slightly. "We're not more than a hundred, two hundred yards from the port." He pointed.

Tynan looked and could see out, over the water. The air was heavy with salt and fish and there was the sound of the ocean lapping at the pilings and docks.

"There a problem?"

"Someone moving over there. Saw one guy and then two more. All of them were armed."

"Maybe local patrol," suggested Tynan.

"Come on, the Cubans took out everyone like that. Got to be Cubans."

"Unless they're our guys."

Hatcher looked toward the harbor again and shook his head. "Our guys are all south of here."

"That's the paratroopers. Maybe some of them landed by sea," said Tynan.

"There any indication that would happen?"

"Hell," said Tynan, "I was as surprised by the paratroopers as you. Nobody told me a thing about that."

"Then we didn't need to come."

Tynan stared at the darkened shape of the sergeant. Tynan knew what the man was saying. Blanchard, Smith and Featherman didn't have to die, if an invasion force was already enroute. That was, if Blanchard and Smith were dead. He didn't know that for sure.

"Let's check it out."

Hatcher nodded and then grabbed Tynan. "Oh, one of those pricks picked up an AK. Wouldn't surrender it and I didn't want to force the issue."

"You tell him not to shoot it?"

"Told him that we had people on the ground here and didn't want him gunning down any Americans. He said that he'd be careful."

Tynan nodded. "You wait here for a moment while I alert Carter."

Hatcher nodded and Tynan ran back to Carter. He told her to hold there for thirty minutes and if they hadn't returned to get the students to the beach and call the sub. She nodded and Tynan headed back to Hatcher.

"Let's do it."

The two of them left the side of the building, crossed the street and ran up a slight incline. From there, the whole port was laid out in front of them. The docks, ships and the lighthouse out on the point were easily visible. Most of the ships were dark with no movement on the decks. The crews had either abandoned them or remained below during the fighting.

Hatcher touched Tynan's sleeve and pointed. There were two men on the dock. One was crouched down, and the other standing.

"What do you think?"

"Let's work our way down there and see who they are."

Hatcher moved first. He stayed close to the top of the hill, just below the rise to conceal himself. Tynan was right behind him. They used a group of bushes and then slipped down to where the dock met the shore. They lay down, prone, watching, but neither of the two men had moved. They stayed where they were, watching the ocean.

Hatcher slipped closer. "What do you make of that?"

"Who knows?"

Two more men suddenly appeared from below the door, climbing up a ladder fastened to one of the pilings. As they reached the dock, one of them turned and pointed back down and said something to the others. There was a burst of laughter and then a fifth man appeared.

"Becoming quite a force," whispered Hatcher.

"Good thing we didn't rush in, guns blazing."

The men stood there and then one of the men picked up a weapon. The distinctive shape gave it away, but that didn't mean much. Tynan was still waiting to hear or see something that would tell them who the men were.

There was a second burst of laughter and then a voice speaking distinctly. "The fucking things at the bottom of the fucking harbor."

"That's it," said Tynan. "They're Americans."

Hatcher started to get up and then flopped down again. "Don't want to surprise them."

Tynan called, "Hey."

The men scattered without a word. Two of them hit the dock, aiming in the general direction of Tynan and Hatcher.

"Four," yelled one of them.

"Numerical code," said Tynan. It meant that he needed to supply a number that would add up to a third number. No one had given them authentication codes because no one had told them there would be other American soldiers on the island.

"Now what?"

Tynan laughed. "Hell, we surrender, of course."

"Of course," said Hatcher.

"Four," came the challenge again.

Tynan shouted, "I am going to stand up slowly. Do not shoot."

"Come ahead," said the voice.

Holding his weapon out to the side where the soldiers on the dock could see it, he stood there and said, "I'm an American naval officer."

"Come forward."

Tynan did as instructed. As he reached the dock, one of the soldiers grabbed the rifle. The man who had been talking to Tynan stood up then and came forward. "What in the hell are you doing here?"

"I was sent in early to get the American students out of the university." He grinned. "We're running late."

"Then where are they?"

"About a hundred yards away, just inside the city." Tynan pointed. "Over there."

"Sarge," yelled the man.

"Get ID."

"Shit," said Tynan. "You don't carry ID on a combat mission."

"I'm afraid that you're going to have to come with us," said the soldier. "Until we can identify you."

"No problem," said Tynan. "Let me get the others over here and you can take us all. I want to get the students out of here as quickly as possible."

"Sarge?"

"Get the students," said the NCO.

"Hatcher," yelled Tynan.

"Who's Hatcher?" asked the soldier.

"My NCO," said Tynan. "Making sure that I haven't gotten myself into trouble."

Now the sergeant came up. He looked at Tynan and said, "You don't have any ID?"

"Not going out on a covert mission."

"Jones. You go with this man and get the students. Bring them back here and we'll decide what to do."

Tynan looked at the NCO and asked, "Let me have my weapon."

The NCO stood there for a moment and then handed it back. "Yes sir."

"Sarge, you're taking a chance here."

"The man's obviously an American so just shut up."

Tynan turned and headed toward Hatcher. As the soldier joined him, he realized that the mission was over. They had gotten the students out and were about to turn them over to someone who could protect them until they could get them off the island.

It was a simple job that had turned bad. Men were dead because no one had told him everything that he needed to know. Secrets had been kept.

They climbed the hill and as they walked down it, the students suddenly came at them. They poured out of the street cheering. They knew that American soldiers were there.

Tynan stood there and watched. Carter finally appeared. Tynan grinned, thinking that she had learned her lessons quickly and well. She waited until she had been sure that everything was under control.

"We did it Jillian," he said as she approached.

She leaped at him, hugging him. "We sure did," she said.

## 19

Standing on the deck of the destroyer, Ed Godwin was looking back toward the island. He, along with Vicki Kehoe and the other American students had been transferred from the shore, from the docks, in a whaleboat that ran out to the task force just outside the harbor. That had been an exciting ride. The harbor was choppy, the salt water splashing up to soak them, but not one of them complained. They had been held by the Cubans, promised rides back to the United States and were now on the way. No one cared that American servicemen had to rescue them. They were just happy to be going home.

Kehoe moved up to where Godwin stood. Over the rumble of the engines, the sound of the sea against the hull of the ship, and the noise drifting toward them from the island, she said, "I will never say a bad thing about the American Army again."

"Why?"

"Because they got us out of there. The Cubans promised to send us home, but they weren't working on it very hard."

"We could have been killed," said Godwin.

"And we could have been shot by the Cubans, just for

being there and in the way. You saw them shooting the injured out there."

"Fighting's still going on. American imperialism at work. A little country that we can overrun," said Godwin ignoring her comment.

She looked at him. Stared at him. "How can you say that? The Cubans invaded first . . ."

Godwin laughed. "Forget it. I was just joking with you." He turned to face her. "I think the Cubans would have released us in time. Let us go. But I don't know. We might have been used as leverage by Castro and his cronies. We'd be released if Washington would agree to such and such. I'm glad to see that it won't happen."

She grabbed his arm and stepped in close, facing him. "Our boys did well, didn't they?"

"Very well. You know how many of them there were?"

"No. How many?"

"If you count that woman, Carter, there were six. Three of them were killed."

"Damn," she said. "I wish that hadn't happened."

"Yeah," agreed Godwin. "I do too." He faced the island again, but it had fallen away. Now there was only a glow in the sky marking the location of Grande Terre. Fires from the fighting that was raging between the Americans, the Cubans, and the local population.

"What are you going to do now?" she asked.

Godwin shook his head. "Hell, we've only been on this ship for two hours. Up until a few hours ago, I was only thinking about getting away from the Cubans before they decided to kill us."

"Me too," Kehoe agreed. "But now we've got to think about the future."

"Why?"

"So that I can . . . I can, well, go to the same school."

"I understand, I guess." He shrugged and looked at her. "I was thinking of applying to a med school in the States, figuring with what I learned here, I might have a better shot at it. At least my test scores will be higher."

"But you're not sure?"

"Or," he said quietly, as if he didn't want her to hear, "I thought about joining the Army. With what I know, I would make a good medic."

She grinned at him. "I was thinking of joining the Army too. Or the Navy. One of the guys who came for us was in the Navy."

"Or the Navy," he agreed. "Right now, I don't know and right now, I don't have to decide."

"Right," she agreed. She was silent for a moment and then added quickly, "But let's do it together."

Godwin didn't answer right away. Then suddenly, he said, "Yeah. Let's do it together." He pulled her close to him and kissed her.

The crew, watching, cheered as that happened.

Tynan, Carter and Hatcher sat in the tiny wardroom of the sub, having been transferred from the destroyer to the sub an hour earlier. They had wiped the psychedelic swirl of camo paint from their faces, though some of it still stained their foreheads near the hairline, stuck to the skin near their ears and could be seen under their chins.

Each of them had a steaming cup of coffee and each of them felt as if they had just been run over by a cement truck. Tynan was leaning back in his chair, feeling more tired than the exertion of the last few hours dictated. He didn't want to do anything and the act of picking up the coffee cup physically drained him.

Carter was the first to break the silence. "Too bad about the others."

"Christ," snapped Tynan. "Too bad. Is that all you can say? That sounds like they fell down and scraped their knees."

She looked at him. "I didn't mean anything . . ."

Tynan felt the pain of leaving his men swell up and overwhelm him. Three men dead. He knew they were dead now. The paratroopers had taken the airfield and found the bodies of Blanchard and Smith near the fence where they had died. They had reported it before Tynan and Hatcher could get back to the airfield.

There was something about the whole situation that angered him. He didn't like abandoning his men, as he had done. When he ordered Hatcher to leave the hangar, he was sure that Blanchard and Smith were dead, but he hadn't known it. Still, there was nothing he could do for them at that point. Had they answered the radio call, had they called for help, that would have been something else.

But the act of leaving them made him feel like a coward. Learning that he had been right, didn't help all that much. Trying to put it out of his mind, he asked Carter, "You know anything about this other mission?"

"No. Nothing."

Hatcher said, "Just like those fuckers at the Pentagon. Everyone has to get into the act." He laughed. "If it hadn't been for us at the airfield, those paratroopers would have been dropped into three anti-aircraft batteries. They'd have been cut to ribbons before they could reach the ground and get into the fight."

Carter snapped her fingers. "Maybe they planned it that way."

"No," said Tynan. "It was only luck that put us on the field when the plane came over. Luck, pure and simple.'

"Dumb fucks," said Hatcher taking a drink of his cof-